—COUSIN—
ONCE REMOVED

—COUSIN—
ONCE REMOVED

Gerald Hammond

St. Martin's Press
New York

Library of Congress Cataloging in Publication Data
Hammond, Gerald.
    Cousin once removed.

    I. Title.
PR6058.A55456C6   1984   823'.914   84-11743
ISBN 0-312-17055-6

First published in Great Britain by Macmillan London Ltd.
First U.S. Edition

10 9 8 7 6 5 4 3 2 1

—COUSIN—
ONCE REMOVED

CHAPTER ONE

A heavily-laden hatchback with a right-hand drive, adhering with great care to the right-hand margin of the road, turned out of the D709 at La Rochebeaucourt on to the D939 and built up speed towards Angoulême.

'I wouldn't say no to the shooting rights around here,' Keith Calder said. He leaned forward to let the breeze from the open window cool the back of the driver's seat. 'You could let out a million pheasants in those woods and they'd stick around.'

'The countryside's just like ours,' Molly said. 'Except for the cover. And the poplars. And the sunflowers.'

'And the heat.'

'The heat isn't so bad, now that we're heading north,' Molly pointed out. 'When'll we get home? The day after tomorrow?'

'Probably.' Keith took his eyes off the road to glance at his wife. Her usually vivacious face looked drawn. 'Are you anxious about Deborah?' he asked.

'She'll be all right with Janet,' Molly said shortly.

Now that it was too late to do anything about it,

Keith could afford to be considerate. 'Not much of a holiday for you, I'm afraid,' he suggested.

'The last week was all right,' Molly admitted. 'But I'm still about worn out.'

'So's the car.'

Keith and Molly Calder had left home nearly seven weeks earlier, intending a fortnight's touring holiday. But, as Keith said, a few business visits would make the whole trip tax-deductible. So they had toured the gun-centre at Liège. Molly had jibbed at the mileage entailed in extending the pilgrimage through Brescia and Burgos. Instead, they had attended auctions and trailed around junk shops in sweltering towns, haggling in a mixture of schoolboy French, pidgin English and sign-language. At first it had seemed that they might get home within a week or ten days of the date they were due. But word had gone round. Keith made friends. Doors had opened which were usually tight shut. A trail had led from one purchase to another. Keith had cabled for more funds. A final week had been spent in a rented farmhouse of golden stone and red pantiles deep in the Dordogne while Keith cleaned, greased, listed and packed his acquisitions and Molly at last found holiday peace in that tranquil countryside. Once, when Keith drove into Bordeaux to enquire about shipping his purchases home, she had gone along to shop. But Bordeaux had been expensive and Keith was already nervous about his own expenditure. Anything that Molly wanted was therefore a drain on after-tax funds. So all that Molly had acquired on her holiday was a deep and beautiful tan – and some French lingerie.

Somehow the question of tax never arose when good French lace was in question.

Molly sighed.

Keith sensed the sigh. 'We can snatch another week in a couple of months' time,' he suggested.

Molly did a quick calculation. Two months would take them into the pheasant season. 'Spend a week beating for you, up to my bum in wet kale? No, thank you very much,' she said. 'Next year Wallace can mind the shop, you can rent Chez Beaudout again and Janet and I can stay there with Deborah while you go off and tour the gunshops on your own.'

'You mean that?' Keith asked, amused.

'Probably not,' Molly admitted. Keith was a good husband and virtuous – when he remembered, which nowadays, Molly admitted to herself, was most of the time. But there had been occasions in the past when his affectionate nature had run away with him.

'Hitch-hiker up ahead,' Keith said, lifting his foot.

'Why this one in particular?'

'She's Scottish.' And indeed the blonde girl had a St Andrew's Cross stitched to her rucksack.

'She also has more tit and bum than she has clothes,' Molly said.

'That's another good reason,' Keith retorted. And Molly gave a quick snort of laughter.

The girl came running up to Keith's window. She had a sulky face but not without prettiness. Her skin was pink rather than brown, turning red at the nose and shoulders. 'Are you going as far as Rouen?' she asked.

'Hop in.' Keith reached back and unlocked the rear door.

The girl slid her brand-new rucksack across the rear seat and ducked inside. 'You're on holiday?'

'Not so's you'd notice,' Molly said. 'And you?'

'Just on the way home. I'm to meet up with friends in Rouen.'

'Where are you from?' Keith asked.

'Glasgow.'

'You don't sound Glasgow.'

'I was brought up in Fife,' she said quickly.

In Angoulême the sign-posting petered out. They threaded their way by a mixture of feminine intuition, male hunch and faint recollections of having once passed that way before, albeit in the opposite direction, and picked up the Poitiers postings. Keith set them moving fast up the N 10.

'Another hitch-hiker,' Molly said. 'A Brit.'

'Sorry, mate,' Keith muttered. 'I have *un petit Froggy* up my tail.' He left the Union Jack, spectacles, teeth, knobbly knees and anxiously waving thumb far behind.

'Seemed like a nice boy,' Molly said.

'I don't pick up nice boys.'

'I noticed. Here's another.'

The next hitch-hiker had the St Andrew's Cross on his rucksack. He seemed about to raise his thumb, then suddenly turned away.

'Did you see that?' Keith said.

'The woodcock? I saw it.'

'Woodcock?' Keith forgot about hitch-hikers.

They made good time through Poitiers and

Châtellerault. Keith turned off the péage into Sainte-Maure-de-Touraine for a quick lunch. They had stayed a night at Le Boule d'Or on the way south. Keith, who loathed getting back into a car which had stood in hot sun, turned up a narrow lane and under the archway into the shaded courtyard.

They were hardly seated before the girl excused herself. She was back within two minutes. 'I've met a friend,' she said. 'It'll be less bother for you if I go on with him. Can I get my rucksack out of your car?'

Keith gave her the key. Keith and Molly had finished eating before they began to wonder why she had not returned it. Keith called for the bill. 'You can pick them, can't you?' Molly said. 'All we need just now's to have the car stolen.'

But the car was still in its patch of shade under the trellis. The doors were unlocked, the key in the ignition. The parcel shelf was in the driver's seat and the interior was in turmoil.

'Turned over, by Christ!' Keith said. 'Shall I get the fuzz?'

'Let's see what we've lost first. If we get the gendarmes we could be here for days.'

Half an hour later Keith closed the last case. He sniffed suspiciously at the necks of his two jerricans and scratched his head. 'If there's anything of mine missing I can't think what the hell it is. Are you short of anything?'

'One bra, but I think I left it on the washing line. It wouldn't have fitted her anyway.'

'Not by a litre or two,' Keith agreed. 'Right. Shall we press on for Dieppe?'

'I'm ready. *En avant!*'

Keith stormed the car out into the main street. There was a shrilling of anguished tyres. 'Keep *right*,' Molly screamed.

By dint of furious driving they caught the last boat of the evening out of Dieppe. They had budgeted for another night in France and were over-provided with francs. Molly was touched when Keith avoided the counter for duty-free drink and instead bought her a large phial of perfume.

They ate dinner. Afterwards they had intended to sleep but instead shared out the remaining francs and settled down to lose them in the company of several compulsive gamblers, in the tiny casino that occupied one wall of the lounge. Keith was soon cleaned out but Molly proved a small but steady winner. The boat came through the Newhaven harbourmouth as she was changing her chips for a useful wad of British notes.

'How come you're always lucky at blackjack?' Keith asked as they descended the stairs to the lower car-deck.

'It's not luck. Wallace told me how to do it. You just never have the biggest bet on the table. The banker plays against the hand with the most money on it, even if it means letting smaller bets win.'

'He never tells me anything useful like that.'

'You never listen to him. But he's an accountant. He *knows* that sort of thing.' They threaded between cars and lorries to where the hatchback stood. Molly stopped dead. 'No!' she wailed. 'Not again!'

This time the hatchback door had been forced. Inside the car the disorder was an exact repetition. Molly, who deplored bad language, uttered a word which she had heard Keith use but which she barely understood.

'Quick,' Keith said. 'Same tidy-up job. Save your opinions for later.'

'Leave it. The cars are beginning to move.'

Keith snorted. 'No way am I driving through customs with the car in this state.'

'And to think that you called me houseproud!'

They set to, forcing clothes and presents back into their cases any old how. When the car in front moved off, Keith pulled his out of the stream of traffic. 'I didn't want to be last off,' he said fretfully. He made a few deft adjustments to the stowage. 'Well, if there's anything missing it can't be anything expensive. You're sure your cameras are all there?'

'Absolutely.'

'Then find me something to tie this door down with.'

They were the last vehicle up the ramp. Keith took the green lane but a customs officer waved him down. 'I said we shouldn't be last,' he whispered. 'They've got time to give the last car the full treatment.' He heaved himself out of the car and untied the half-a-pair-of-tights which held the hatchback door shut, keeping up a constant grumble about the damage while the bored man poked through their luggage, sniffed at Keith's two jerricans and glanced disapprovingly at the bottles displayed on the back seat.

11

Five minutes later they were pulling out of Newhaven's one-way circuit. A heavy lorry bore down on them with horn blaring and lights ablaze. 'Keep left,' Molly screamed.

Keith jerked the car across the road. The lorry howled angrily past. Keith smoothed out his swerve and pretended that it had never happened. 'Shall we drive right through?' he suggested. 'Get home in time for lunch?'

'Yes, let's. If you're fit to get us past London you can sleep while I take us up the motorways.' Molly patted his knee. 'You can't wait to see Deborah again either, can you?'

'Of course not.' Keith hid a yawn. It was his dogs in their boarding kennel that were uppermost in his mind.

In Scotland there was what passed for a heatwave, but the Calders found it cool after the sun of southern France. They breezed along until at last they turned down off the main road and Keith drove through the town of Newton Lauder and out to Briesland House, their home. They ate, bathed and changed before heading back into the town. They had slept in turns on the long road north. Molly was drowsy but Keith had come alert again.

They parked in the quiet square, almost outside the shop with its black fascia and elegant gold lettering – Keith Calder & Co. Underneath, in very small letters, it added 'Gunsmith to Royalty', on the strength of an emergency repair once carried out to the drilling belonging to a remote relative of ex-King Zog. Nobody had ever objected.

While Molly, softly cooing, fled upstairs to renew acquaintance with her only child, Keith sidled into the shop to face his partner.

One look at Wallace James's long, bony face told Keith that his partner was understandably peevish. Keith would also have known this by the absence of Wallace's slight stammer, which disappeared miraculously in moments of anger. Wallace's first words made his sentiments clear. 'You go and bugger off,' he said, 'for a short holiday abroad, leaving me to look after the business, my wife to bring up your family and Molly's brother to look after your home and garden, and you stay gone for about two bloody months! And we'd hardly have known you were still alive but for regular demands for more and more money.'

'I've spent a bit,' Keith admitted, 'but I've spent it well.'

'So as well as being overdrawn again we're also overstocked?'

'I can turn this lot over for a hell of a profit,' Keith said.

Wallace was slightly appeased. 'Just as long as you do turn them over,' he said. 'I don't want them going plop into your personal collection and getting stuck there.'

'I don't have a personal collection.'

'Then why's the best specimen of each type always priced at more than it could ever fetch?'

They were interrupted in this long-running argument by the arrival of a prospective customer, a young man with pink skin and a leather hat who turned away to the rack of trout rods. 'Just browsing,' he said.

Wallace returned his attention to Keith. 'All right, then. What did you bring back?'

'Not to say bring back, because I bought about forty guns. The car couldn't have pulled a load like that and I didn't want a hassle with the customs. That's why we spent the last week at Verteillac, listing and packing them for consignment. I sent them by coaster, so God knows when they'll fetch up. All I brought back with me was a bottle of Médoc for you. Not a well-known château but I think you'll like it.'

Wallace's manner showed a nice mixture of gratitude and irritation. 'Very good of you,' he said stiffly, 'but not the cleverest use of your duty-free allowance.'

Keith shrugged and smiled. 'I'll be the judge of that. If I can't do a favour for a friend. . . .'

'We'll d-drink it together. Now, tell me about the trip.'

'It was just great,' Keith said. 'I thought the country had been picked clean, but I managed to pick up a few good pieces in need of restoration. Somebody told me that Monsieur Becquet of the Armurerie Central in Riberac had a stock of bits and pieces, so I called on him and he produced boxes of old hammers and things. I wanted to buy the lot but he'd only sell individual items, which is why we spent a week nearby, matching up missing hammers and so on. Anyway, he put me on to a collector near St Aulaye who wanted to sell some things to raise cash for a sale that was coming up in Bordeaux.'

14

'Aha!' Wallace said. He hunted in a drawer under the counter and produced a press cutting. 'That'll be how this came about. It was in *The Scotsman* about a fortnight ago.'

Keith read:

PISTOLS COMING HOME

A rare pair of Scottish duelling pistols, made by Ross of Edinburgh and dating from about 1830, will soon be returning to Scotland after an absence of many years.

COACH IN BARN

The pistols, described as percussion and with three-quarter stocks and octagonal barrels, are in the original case. They were found in a coach which was itself discovered by masons demolishing an old barn near Libourne, France. The coach, for no known reason, had been walled up in the end of the barn.

The coach, said to be in 'remarkably good condition', will go to the Musée des Artes in Bordeaux. The pistols came under the hammer in an auction last Wednesday at the Galleries Ramboult, also in Bordeaux. They were bought by Mr Keith Calder of Newton Lauder, for the equivalent of £85.

'Eighty-five quid doesn't seem much for a good pair of duellers,' Wallace remarked.

'They're pretty badly rusted,' Keith said, 'but they should clean up. There was some rare stuff in

15

that sale, Wal, but most of it fetched far too much. Quite a few of the guns were British – the whole region's riddled with English names. It belonged to the English Crown until the middle of the fifteenth century, but there was a special trading relationship for a hell of a time after that.

'Anyway, my collector got what he was after and he made up the money by selling me a duck's-foot pistol, slightly damaged, and a double-barrel French flintlock of Wender type – you know, Wal, the barrels turn over – and it's in good enough nick for a museum, except that the engraving verges on the pornographic.

'And at the sale a French artisan type came and spoke to me. Well, I'd been getting by in schoolboy French with a few technical terms thrown in, but this old boy spoke a strong patois filtered through solid garlic. We managed to understand each other with a little help from the rest of the crowd who all joined in. I'd just discovered that if you pick the English word that sounds most likely to have come from the French, and use it, they may laugh but they'll understand it.'

'The trouble with you,' Wallace said, 'is that you get so damned *interested* in things.'

'Maybe,' Keith said without really hearing. 'It turned out that he was foreman of the gang that had found the coach and they were in for a share of whatever the pistols fetched. He wasn't too disappointed with the price – it was all found money to them – so he wanted to buy me a drink. In the end he took me out to see the place – not exactly a château, more an old, up-market farmhouse.'

'Why would anyone want to wall up a pair of Scottish pistols in a coach in a French barn?' Wallace asked.

'I don't know, and I'm not particularly bothered. If you want to puzzle your head over it, you may as well know that the coach was Scottish too, and the same crest was on the panels as on the gate-posts of the place. Figure that one out. Old Jules Michelet was a gem. We got on like brothers. But, Christ, how that man could drink! We got stoned together for about three days and Molly hasn't forgiven me yet. They have sort of fermented prunes over there that can just about blow your head off. I brought a jar of them back for Ronnie and we'll see what he makes of them. The customs man looked at them a bit oddly, but he let them by.

'I'd been browsing round the shops and the dealers, but old Jules tapped me straight into the peasant network. "You go and see old so-and-so," he'd say. "He's got his grandfather's musket hanging over the fireplace." And when I'd bought old so-and-so's grandad's musket, old so-and-so would pass me along to a neighbour whose great-uncle had been gamekeeper to Richelieu's nephew or something. Those peasants hate to lose anything. I came across a few guns which had been hidden away from the Nazis during the war and never taken out again. One old boy had an Alexander Forsyth shotgun by Joe Manton which had been converted, very crudely, to percussion-cap, and Molly spotted the original scent-bottle primer on a shelf in the barn.'

The customer nodded and left the shop. Wallace hardly saw him go. 'F-first or second model?' he asked keenly.

'First.'

'Well, all right. It d-doesn't sound as if you've wasted much of the firm's t-time or money, so I'm not quite as furious as I was. Have you,' Wallace asked sternly, 'got every bill and receipt for the taxman?'

Keith nodded several times. 'Every last one. Would I have dared face you if I hadn't?'

'You might have t-tried.'

'I'd have sent Molly to break it to you. Now, I've got a couple of calls to make. If Molly looks for me, tell her I'll be back shortly. And I must get down to preparing a catalogue of those guns.'

'First things first,' Wallace said. 'There's a dozen or more guns in for overhaul, all wanted in time for the grouse.'

'They'll get them in time for the pheasants.'

'Split the difference,' Wallace said. 'Partridges. How did you get on driving in France?'

'They were all driving on the wrong side, but I soon sorted them out,' Keith said. 'See you!'

Newton Lauder's premier wine merchant was situated only a few yards from Keith's shop, but Keith had no special contact with its proprietor. For this errand he needed a friend. He drove several streets north and west to where, among the more expensive houses of the town, he could park outside what was little more than a very superior off-licence. Andy Coutts, the owner, was a vintage arms enthusiast and a regular customer at the shop.

Keith carried his bottles inside and set them on the counter. 'Horse-trading time, Andy,' he said.

Andy Coutts studied the bottles. 'Champagne cognac!' he said. He referred to a tome on the counter. 'I can give you a damn good trade on these. You'd a good holiday?'

'Just grand! And while I was looking around I remembered you turning out with a Le Page shotgun, and the hammers not matching.' Keith took a small object from his pocket and laid it beside his bottles. 'Don't lay a finger on it yet, but would that not make a better match?'

Coutts's eyes lit up. His hand moved but stopped at Keith's headshake. 'It would.'

'I could make it so's you'd not know the difference. Now, bide a wee minute. Look but don't touch.'

Keith went out to his car and took out his two jerricans. From the mouth of each he tipped out a gill or so of liquid into the gutter. With a damp cloth he wiped carefully round the neck of the can marked 'Petrol' before carrying both inside. On the counter, he picked away with his knife at the wax seals round the black plastic cups in the necks of the cans, and picked the cups out. 'Here you are,' he said. 'Eight gallons of good claret, straight from the vineyard in the Médoc. Personal stock of the proprietor, who was selling me a miquelet at the time. He'd half-promised it to somebody else who hadn't come up with the money. It was in rather tatty condition, so I made him throw in the wine.' The value of the wine was included in the receipt for the gun, but Wallace need never know.

19

'I'm in no position to bottle that kind of stuff,' Coutts protested.

'You deal with the hotels. Sell it to them for table carafes.'

'You could sell it to them yourself.'

'I'm not wanting to sell it, I'm wanting to swap it. That way it needn't figure in anybody's books. But if I swapped it with a hotel I'd have to take their booze at hotel prices.'

Silence fell between them. Through the shop's window Keith admired the figure of a red-haired girl who was pricing the wines on display.

'Well, I don't know,' Coutts said slowly.

'All right.' Keith picked up the hammer. 'If you don't want to oblige me. . . .'

'I didn't say I wouldn't,' Coutts said hastily. 'Just what sort of a deal did you have in mind?'

'Start with a bottle of Médoc for my partner. Something cheap that he wouldn't recognize the name of.'

Twenty minutes of hard bargaining later, Keith fitted the last case of beer into the back of the car. He stood back to admire the stack of assorted alcohols, almost into the path of a passing Capri. 'And every drop of it duty-free,' he told himself. 'Accountants don't know everything.'

He drove off to collect his dogs.

CHAPTER TWO

Holidays, even holidays taken on money never shared with the Inspector of Taxes, have to be paid for in other ways. Wallace's wife, Janet, was adamant that, after holding the fort for so long, she and Wal were going to have a break of their own and they were going to have it before the shooting season opened and thereafter took up all of the men's time until late the following February. She took a reluctant Wallace off to visit an aunt in Fort William.

With a lot of help from Minnie Pilrig, their occasional assistant, and such time as Molly could spare from house and baby, Keith found himself running the shop, overtaking the backlog of gun repairs, preparing his catalogue and coping, in such time as he could spare, with his own specialized branch of the business, which was dealing in antique weapons and appurtenances and modern replicas thereof. All this he managed to do by keeping up a furious pace through rather more hours than God had ever allocated for work until, as he said, he would have been fresher if he had never gone on holiday at all.

'I could have done with a holiday myself,' Molly pointed out.

'Am I very inconsiderate?'

She gave him a kiss on the ear which sent a jolt straight to his vital organs. 'I never expected anything else,' she said.

And so he slogged on for ten hard days.

On the eleventh, Molly was taking care of the shop while Minnie Pilrig tended the needs of her own family. Keith's workbench, together with the antiques side of the business, had years before been squeezed out of the shop by the expansion of retail trade under Wallace's management. So it was on the first floor of Briesland House, among the racked weapons of older days, that Keith was working on the more modern guns when Molly telephoned. He turned the Vivaldi tape down to a whisper.

'Sir Henry Batemore just rang,' Molly said. She sounded awed. 'He wants you to go and see him.'

'At Wallengreen Castle?'

'Yes.'

'What about?'

'He didn't say. He just said to be there at twelve.'

'Call him back. Tell him to come here. I'll see him at two sharp.'

'Keith!' Molly was shocked. 'You can't do that. He's important.'

'Not to me, he isn't. He doesn't shoot and I never heard of him owning anything worth having in the way of guns. He fishes, but he never puts any business our way. The hell with him.'

'But, Keith, isn't he Home Secretary or something?'

'Something. He's Shadow Home Secretary. There's a difference. He isn't even our MP. . . . And his son's one of those hunt saboteurs. I'm not driving thirty miles each way because Sir Henry crooks a finger.'

'Well, I'm not calling him back to say so.'

'Molly, I'm *busy!*'

'You want to insult the Shadow Home Secretary, you call him back. I've got customers in the shop.' She hung up.

Keith glared at the phone while his hands resumed dismantling an Anson and Deeley action. When it came down to it, he was chary of antagonizing an influential man and potential customer and one, moreover, who might have considerable clout with the police after the next election. He relieved his feelings with the rudest word which, for the moment, came into his mind. The gun retorted by flicking its top-lever spring over his shoulder and into the darkest corner of the room.

Twelve noon was already past when Keith turned his car through the gates of Wallengreen Castle. For this the labyrinthine roads which thread the lusher plain near the English border, and a system of sign-posting which seemed to assume that he already knew the way, were to blame.

Scotland teems with castles, many of them reminders of a war-torn history. Some are ruins. Some, because any man may call his home a castle, are little more than minor country houses with a token battlement or two. Others are almost fortified palaces. Wallengreen Castle was no Victorian fantasy but a sizeable sixteenth-century stronghold which had been modernized as far as was essential for comfortable living and not an inch beyond. The work had been done with taste and a respect for the old structure, and the result was that the building had a strange, grim charm like, Keith thought, a murderous teddybear.

Keith parked on gravel, climbed granite steps and thumbed a modern bell-push. The heavy outer doors were already open. There was movement beyond an inner, glazed screen and a butler opened its door. Keith was not unacquainted with butlers; indeed, at one time the butler to a noble but impoverished household had come poaching with him regularly, strictly for his lordship's table. This butler, however, was large, portly, pompous and attired in the height of formality and discomfort – and apparently proud of it. Keith disliked him on sight.

Keith produced his business card. The butler examined it as if it had been a dead mouse. 'The tradesmen's entrance is at the back,' he said.

'I don't give a hoot where it is. I come in this way or not at all,' Keith said slowly and distinctly.

The butler blinked at him. 'Round the back,' he repeated.

'Goodbye,' Keith said. He turned and descended the steps towards his car.

The butler followed him as far as the head of the steps. 'Where are you going?'

'I'm going home. I'll write to Sir Henry and tell him why. And I'll tell him that if he still wants the favour of an interview he can make a fresh appointment and come to my shop at my convenience. And a bloody good day to you too!'

The butler squared himself for battle and then suddenly capitulated. 'Come this way, please,' he said.

Keith followed a back which radiated injured dignity, through the two sets of doors, across a hallway and up a twisting flight of stairs into a gallery. This was lit by large windows of comparatively recent date, looking on to a courtyard or bailey bright with flowers. In keeping with the building's original purpose most of the windows, old and new, overlooked the courtyard and Keith could easily have skimmed a quick impression of the interior workings of the castle. But the other long wall of the gallery was racked with row upon row of guns. Keith almost stopped in his tracks but walked on, using his eyes. The butler opened a heavy door at the far end.

'Mr Calder,' he announced and stood back.

Keith moved forward and heard the door close behind him. Sir Henry was writing at an ornate desk and did not look up. Keith did not expect him to – he knew how the game was played. He seated himself on a tapestry chair and looked round the book-lined room.

Out of the corner of his own eye he could see the other man surreptitiously eyeing him. Sir Henry Batemore was in his early fifties. He had been of middle build before he had begun to spread about the belly. His face was flattened, reminding Keith of a Pekinese. His eyes were watery and seemed slightly bloodshot. All in all, an undistinguished and puffy set of features was saved from absolute mediocrity by a crown of prematurely white hair which looked very well on television and by the deeply resonant orator's voice which had been his major political asset.

'Do sit down.'

'I already did,' Keith pointed out.

'Yes.' Sir Henry nodded in forgiveness of the presumption. 'You may be wondering why I sent for you.'

'I am.'

'Mr Calder, you have just returned from abroad where you purchased a number of antique guns.'

'I know,' Keith said.

'There is no need to take that tone,' said the mellifluous voice. 'I am merely opening up the subject. Mr Calder, I want first refusal of any of the guns which you brought back with you.'

Keith thought, and then shook his head.

'Mr Calder, I intend to have it.' Years in high office seemed to have convinced Sir Henry that a demand made loudly enough and in an Oxford accent was bound to be acceded to. But he did not know Keith Calder.

'Why should I give you preference over my other customers?' Keith asked. 'And, anyway, which one do you want?'

'I'm not prepared to tell you which one. I've no intention of being held to ransom.'

Keith decided that he was going to nail Sir Henry's hide to the barn door. 'No way am I going to give you first pick if I don't know what you want. Why don't you buy the whole lot?'

'How much?'

'Say . . . twelve grand.'

'That's blackmail?'

'Balls,' Keith said sweetly. 'You should know the meaning of the word blackmail. After all, it originated hereabouts, possibly it was first said either by or about the laird of this very place. If you buy them from me and let me resell the ones you don't want on your behalf, you might well end up showing a profit.'

Sir Henry thought it over for a few seconds and then shook his head. 'I'd have to place too much trust in your integrity and your judgment.' He paused and a glint came into his eye. 'Now, suppose I were to offer you your choice of any five of the guns outside in exchange for, say, any two of yours.'

Keith realized that, although he disliked Sir Henry and all that he stood for—including Parliament —they nevertheless had some common ground. Each was a natural higgler in the market place. He settled down to enjoy himself. 'You had your butler whip me through there in about ten seconds flat,' he said. 'You wanted to whet my interest without giving me time to study them. Well, I don't need half that time to get the general picture. Any valuable guns out there were sold many years back. Maybe times were hard. Then times got better and your interior decorator or your wife or somebody filled up the blank space by buying in guns. But they're like your books in here, bought by the yard for the sake of the bindings.'

'You're going out of your way to be insulting,' Sir Henry said, although he looked faintly amused.

'If you want to tell me that you read theology in German to get to sleep,' Keith said, 'go ahead and try to convince me. Those guns outside comprise about a hundred Tower muskets, probably bought when the Tower of London was selling them off for a few quid each. They fetch a bit more now, but they're still the commonest flintlock going, and that number would be a drag on the market. Then, just to add a little variety, twenty-odd clapped-out hammer-guns of rockbottom quality have been thrown in. And even those have probably been picked over by some dealer.'

'A friend of my son bought one,' Sir Henry admitted. 'But the man's a rank amateur. There could still be something worth having.'

'There is. Two that I noticed. There might be more. I don't think so, but there might. If I go and look I'll have a better idea whether I can meet you.'

Sir Henry hesitated and then nodded. He began to get up.

'No,' Keith said firmly. 'I'm not having you looking over my shoulder. If I trade in the dark, then so do you.' He walked out into the gallery, closing the door behind him. Although he was almost certain that nobody was watching, he spread his attention over the whole collection. How the hell had a Maynard tape-primer got in among that collection of rubbish? And how had a collector of even modest competence missed it? The Frazer shotgun was understandable – it had been crudely converted from pinfire to centrefire. He returned to the study.

'Well?'

'Just the two. One good, one moderate.'

'Which two?'

'Uh-uh,' Keith said. 'For that kind of advice I charge a fee. I wouldn't want them disappearing to Christie's.'

'You can trust me.'

'I'm sure of it,' Keith said. 'But your profession's against you.'

For the first time, Sir Henry Batemore threw back his head and laughed. Like Keith, he was enjoying the battle of wits. 'I suppose it is at that! Well, make me a proposition.'

Keith could make a very good guess as to what Sir Henry was after. 'Without having the faintest idea what you're after,' he said, 'my hands are tied. But try this for size. We might have a deal if I could be sure you weren't after any of the more valuable guns I'm bringing back. Can I take it that you're not interested in a French matchlock with matching musket-rest? Or an early Dutch snaphaunce, showing a bulge deriving from the wheel-lock? Or a duck's-foot pistol?' While he spoke, Keith was watching the other's eyes.

But Sir Henry looked away. 'Oh no, you don't,' he said. 'I might just as well tell you aloud which ones I want. Let's try it another way. I'll trust you this far. If you were out to buy my two guns, what would you offer?'

Keith named a figure.

'Right,' Sir Henry said. 'When your guns reach your shop, you let me know. I'll meet you there. I'll buy what I want at your list price, and provided that I'm the first customer to see any of your guns, you

29

can buy my two for half your figure. How does that sound?'

Keith looked over Sir Henry's left shoulder and kept expression off his face. The deal sounded good. He had pitched the value of Sir Henry's guns low; and he was sure that he knew what the other wanted and could therefore inflate the value. Sir Henry was ready to shake hands and Keith was tempted to clinch the deal. But his curiosity, which Molly called his hunter's instinct, was against such an inconclusive outcome. Also, a still better deal might come along. And Sir Henry had a son whom Keith had never met and yet despised. Finally, Keith had been directed to the tradesmen's entrance.

Keith never went back on his word. So he decided not to give it. 'I've already had enquiries from some of my best customers, following that piece in *The Scotsman*,' he said. Sir Henry's eyes shifted focus at the mention. 'I don't want to offend any of them. If I let you jump the queue you'll have to throw those two guns in for free.'

The Shadow Home Secretary gave Keith a glare which reminded him of a muzzle-flash at dusk. By now Keith could read him like a book. Sir Henry loved to do a deal but disliked parting with money or money's worth. Mean or not, he was determined. 'Very well,' he said. 'We have a deal.'

'I'll sleep on it,' Keith said. 'Good morning to you.'

Keith slaved through the following weekend, fretful at being confined to the house while the weather held fair. On the Sunday night Wallace and Janet returned and took over the shop and, for two more days, Keith concentrated on clearing the backlog of guns for overhaul or repair. By Wednesday morning he was struggling with the last, a Darne which showed that most malignant of maladies – occasional misfiring while seeming to be mechanically perfect. He traced the deformed component at last and was assembling the gun for, he hoped, the last time when the telephone gave its double shrill. He turned Mozart off.

'Calder.'

A man's voice came on the line. A young man, Keith judged from the tone. 'Mr Calder? This is Brian Batemore. You don't know me, but –'

Keith sighed and broke in. 'Your old man's been on the phone to me every day for nearly a week. Tell him I'm still not prepared to commit myself.'

'It's not that,' the voice said quickly. 'It's more . . . personal.'

'Hold on.' Unseen, Keith smiled. He put down the turnscrew in his hand and took the phone over to the window. He fetched the litre bottle of Guinness which had been awaiting his attention and settled down in his worn armchair ready for a long chat. There were worse ways to pass the time than to look out over his sunlit garden while riding, metaphorically speaking, one of his many hobbyhorses. 'I'll be as personal as you bloody like,' he said, 'and you can hang up any time you want. I've been seeing your name in the papers from time to time, and from what I read you're a prick of the first water, you and your Hunt Saboteurs' Association.

31

Me, I don't give a fart for hunting. I've told the Master often enough that if he wants to justify the hunt's existence they've got to be seen as an effective method of fox-control; but they'd rather leave plenty of foxes on the ground for the sake of their next day out. They expect everyone else to leave their foxes alone and never mind how many chickens or lambs or game-birds they kill.'

'Well, then—'

'But you, you're worse,' Keith said. 'You can still hang up whenever you like. I'll say this for the hunt. No fox, chopped by hounds, lives for more than a second, despite what your propaganda makes out, and I don't know any other method of control which can be counted on to be anything like that quick, not even lamping with a rifle. And the hunt is pursuing a perfectly legitimate activity. You and your rabble break the law to interfere with that activity and you don't care a drop of bat-piss for the fox. You're acting out of malice, and then preying on class-hatred and the sympathy of the ignorant when you get your smelly little arses into trouble. To my mind, if it's all right for you to break the law because you don't approve of hunting, then it's fair enough for the hunt supporters to knock seven colours of shit out of you when they catch you at it.'

He paused for a sip of his Guinness. He could hear a faint, whispered colloquy at the other end. 'Finished?' asked the voice. It sounded amused.

Keith decided that this was a subject on which he could speak for three minutes or for three hours but not for any period in between. 'For the moment,' he said.

'Well, I've heard you out. Now, you owe me a listen. You know the Foleyhill Nature Reserve?'

Keith did. 'Don't call it a nature reserve,' he said. 'That implies some sort of official status. Call it a sanctuary, if you must dignify it. I didn't know you had anything to do with Foleyhill.'

When the man spoke again there was an exaggerated patience in his voice. 'The Foleyhill sanctuary, then. And you know now. We've got a problem out there.'

'It's a problem you're making for everybody else,' Keith said. He was off again. In addition to his strong feelings on the subject, he was remembering other reasons for disliking Sir Henry's son. He was, for instance, on Wallace's list of Cash Only customers. Keith made a mental note to ask Wal whether this denoted insolvency, disapproval or merely the suspicion than any animal rights crank would be unlikely to settle a debt to a gunshop. 'You and your kind,' he went on, 'you've been brainwashed by Walt Disney. You expect all God's creatures to snuggle up together. What you've done is to provide a safe haven for foxes, carrion crows and every other dam predator. So there's damn-all else in your bloody sanctuary and your vermin goes raiding over the boundaries for food. The shoot on Fallowfield had to cut down on their pheasant releasing by five hundred this year, because it wasn't worth rearing more chicks than they could protect, just to feed your wildlife. So that's five hundred creatures, thanks to you and your sanctuary, which don't get a chance of life in the wild. And a good chance, too, because they never did recover more than forty per cent in a good year.'

'We might be agreeable to a planned programme of control,' said the voice.

'You what?'

'Some of our members are arguing that nature needs a bit of a hand to keep her balance. We've been doing a bird-count and we don't like the answers much. We might look for help in a control programme if you'll advise us about something else.'

This sudden reversal of entrenched attitudes took Keith's breath away. He was silent until the voice at the other end asked anxiously, 'Are you there?'

'I'm here,' Keith said. 'What did you want advice about?'

'Roe deer.'

'Ah. From what I hear, that's a different matter. You seem to have a small number of bucks, each holding a good-sized territory for himself, his doe and her fawns. The surplus population are pushed out into the moor and the farmland, where there's inadequate cover for them. The farmers aren't any too pleased, but it makes for good stalking for the rest of us. And the population occupying the forestry on Foleyhill should be at an acceptable level. What's your problem?'

'Two problems. The owner's getting uptight about damage to trees by the roe. And we think we've got a poacher.'

'That's not so good. The cure is a winter cull of does. But if the poacher knocks off the territorial bucks, you'll get an increased population and a lot more fraying damage while the territory's in dispute. Roe damage isn't always as bad as it looks. And roe aren't always guilty of what they're blamed for. You'd better get expert advice.'

'Would you come out and look at it for us?'

Keith hesitated. He knew the ground well, had shot the farms round about and even poached occasionally in wilder days. A guided tour might be interesting and even useful. On the other hand, he was a busy man. 'Why not try my brother-in-law?' he asked. 'He knows more about roe deer than they know about themselves.'

The voice did not seem to have a high opinion of Keith's brother-in-law. 'Ronnie Fiddler,' it said, 'is an arrogant, pig-headed, bigoted oaf.'

'You know him? Get him to help.'

'Only by reputation. You're less biased –'

Keith laughed. 'You can say that after the tongue-lashing I just gave you?'

'That might have put me off if I hadn't heard you speak and read your articles. Ecology, conservation and so on. Okay, so you sound off a bit. But at least you see both sides. Most people take up extreme views and stick to them. So what do you say? Will you come and take a look with me?'

Keith glanced round at his workbench. It looked unappealing. Outside, the sun was shining and there was a cooling breeze. On the lawn, Molly was teaching Deborah to walk with the dogs in anxious attendance. It was a cosy and tranquil scene and Keith would have liked to join it. But the dogs needed something more robust in the way of exercise if they were to be fit for the hard work to

35

come. The spaniel, Tanya, especially – it would probably be her last working season, poor old thing. And, Keith admitted to himself, he too could do with some exercise. It had been a sedentary summer.

'Give me time to eat,' he said. 'Could you pick me up around two? My wife may need the car.'

There was another outbreak of whispering. 'I'm pushed for transport myself,' said the voice. 'I may have to be dropped.'

'All right,' Keith said. 'I'll meet you at the old quarry about two-thirty.'

He hung up. He slapped the Darne back together, hoping for the best, and went to find his walking boots.

CHAPTER THREE

The area known as Foleyhill is something of a geological oddity. Situated where the fertile plain of the south-east Border country begins to merge with the tract of undulating moorland beyond which lies Newton Lauder, Foleyhill bulges like a wart on an angel's nose, a few square miles of broken, rocky ground, unfit for cultivation except for a few areas of forestry.

After a mile on an unmade road Keith came to the old quarry. It seemed to be deserted.

A shoulder of discoloured stone had been left protruding from the wing of the quarry, but Keith knew from earlier, illicit visits that a track ran round the shoulder to where a second, smaller face had once been opened. Looking for a cool place to park, he reversed his car round into the track, parking where he sensed the shade would reach within an hour or so. Somebody had been less patient or would need his car again sooner, for Keith could see a headlamp and a rim of dark blue wing further round the curve. He let the dogs out of their bed in the hatchback's boot. The young labrador romped ahead of him back to the quarry, but the old spaniel took her time, working the stiffness out of her bones.

Keith had not heard another car, but a young man in a fringed shirt and leather hat was waiting in the quarry.

'Mr Batemore?' Keith asked.

'Mr Calder?'

Neither man offered to shake hands.

'I've seen you around Newton Lauder,' Keith said, 'but I didn't know who you were.'

'It was good of you to come, but we don't exactly encourage dogs in the . . . sanctuary.'

'They're trained gundogs. They won't disturb game, if you have any, unless I tell them to. And unless and until you get an interdict I can walk them through here any time I want to.'

'All right. You don't have to be so scratchy. Just as long as they behave. We'll walk this way and I'll show you some of the problems.'

A second track, little more than a path, led from the end of the road over a low hump of rocky ground and down between two plantations of conifers. They turned off and followed a small stream to where it emerged into low, damp ground.

'Here's some of the damage.'

Keith squatted and examined the damage to the small trees with care. He sniffed the bark. 'You can tell your landlord, or whoever it is that's kicking up about the damage, that you've got voles – here at least. Show me some more.'

They squelched through the boggy ground and Keith said, 'You ought to have snipe here. You would have, given a little work and some dung to encourage the invertebrates.'

38

They studied another area of vole-damage. Keith looked up the long slope to where Foleyhill was crowned by more forestry and a mixed copse of large hardwoods. 'There used to be tawny owls up there. Are they still around?'

'They are. And no way do you get to shoot them.'

Keith sighed. 'I wouldn't wish to,' he said. 'If you want to be a conservationist you'd better learn a little about ecology. Let the forces of nature do the work. The owls could control the voles for you, but they don't like covering long distances without a perch. Try putting in a line of posts down the hill for them to perch on. When they find there's a supply of voles down here, they won't have to hit the other birds so hard up at the top. Now, come over here.' Keith led the other man to a tree which shone whitely, stripped of bark to a height of three feet. The ground beneath it was scuffed. 'This is a roe-buck's "fraying-stock", sort of boundary marker. But it's the only one I can see.'

They set off on a diagonal climb up the slope. After a hundred yards Keith stopped and looked down on top of the plantations. 'You can see the feeding-damage from here,' he said. 'It's not very much and it's evenly distributed. The extra growth on the neighbouring trees would just about make up the difference.' They climbed again. The rocky slope had a cover of old heather. 'There's plenty of grit,' Keith said, 'and the choice of two streams. If you did some heather-burning – in small patches, mind – you could have grouse here.'

'And every poacher for miles around.'

'What, for God's sake, is the good of having a sanctuary and then saying you don't want birds in it in case they attract poachers?'

'You may have a point there.'

They reached the trees near the first crest. The dogs were panting like steam-engines and the two men were sweating so that midges made a cloud around them. 'A place like this should deafen you with birdsong,' Keith said. 'And it still could, if you let some sunlight in to encourage the underbrush and got somebody to thin out the crows and magpies, and maybe the foxes. Chrissake, you've got fewer wild creatures here than down on the farmland.'

'There's something I want to show you over here,' the young man said.

They walked through the deep shade, silent on the accumulated leaf-mould, sometimes scrambling over loose boulders. Towards the further margin of the trees were some natural clearings and here they followed a deer-track through bracken and nettles. A lonely blackbird gave his alarm-call. The last clearing opened out on to a view over a hundred square miles of moor and farmland.

'What do you make of this?'

From a limb of a large tree hung the carcass of a roe-doe. A start had been made to slitting the belly but it seemed that the poacher had been interrupted. Keith stood and looked at it from a few yards away. 'Shot by a crossbow,' he said. 'The bolt's still in it. Out of season too. Something must have frightened him off.'

'There's no crossbow here.' The young man sounded puzzled.

'Well, there wouldn't be, would there?'

'There was one nearby when we – I – found it this morning.'

Keith thought back to his own youth. 'My guess would be that he was starting to gralloch the deer when he heard you coming. He ducked into cover. As soon as you'd gone he retrieved the crossbow. But he wouldn't want to be caught with it on him. Maybe he hid it and hasn't come back for it yet. We'd better take a look around.'

'I suppose so. Seems a pity to waste the meat, once it's been killed. Couldn't you. . . ?'

'Hardly worth it,' Keith said. 'It's been left too long. The blood will have set into jelly by now. Still, I suppose it would feed the dogs.'

He pulled his knife from his belt and put a hand on the carcass. The young man took several steps to one side, as if he were afraid of being splashed with blood.

A movement, seen from the corner of his eye, made Keith turn his head. A girl had come out of the trees. She had red hair and a dark tan, which looked wrong to Keith's eye – in his experience, red hair went with a pale skin that seldom tanned well. She wore the same kind of cowboy hat as the young man. No, he corrected himself. Not cowboy. The kind of leather hat which was sold in all the markets in France.

And she was pointing a camera at him.

As the implication of the camera rammed past all the others, Keith ducked away to hide his face. And

41

in that moment came a noise. He was struck an appalling blow on and in and through the right shoulder. He was unconscious before he hit the ground.

Some time later, perhaps an hour but he never found out, Keith drifted back to the surface of consciousness. He was lying in the same place, in a pool of his own blood which hummed with a thousand flies. A rough bandage seemed to have been tied round his shoulder and around the arrow which still transfixed it. Between shock and the effect of loss of blood he was incapable of making sense of these circumstances. Although he was lying in the sun the world looked grey and he was aware of a deep cold. The rasping flannel on his face he recognized as the tongue of the younger dog, the black labrador, which had been licking anxiously at his face but now sat back, conscious of a job well done. The older dog, the liver-and-white springer, lay a few yards off, whining occasionally but awaiting his command.

Through the fog which clouded his brain Keith thought that he could hear men's voices. He tried to raise himself but a tearing pain, worse than anything in his life before, flashed from his right shoulder through his whole being, and although he did not know it, he began to bleed again. He opened his mouth to shout. He managed only a croak but that was enough to raise the agony again. Consciousness faded away and then returned, palely. The voices were there still, but fainter. He thought that they were further away, but he could not be sure.

A weight of many tons had dragged his eyelids shut. He pulled them open by brute force. Another pair of eyes stared unblinking into his own. Tanya, the old springer spaniel, boon companion on a thousand forays, was almost retired from active work. She lay stretched full length. Her muscles were taut and quivering. She was waiting for the word but she knew better than to set off without it.

Keith fought aside the cotton-wool mists which blew across his mind. He had no strength to lift a hand. He managed a movement of one finger, a flick with his eyes and the merest breath of a whisper and let his eyes close. He was not sure that he had made any sound at all. But when he forced his eyelids open again the spaniel was gone. He thought, as he faded away again, that he had heard the yip which she always gave when she got up after sitting, when her stiff joints pained her. But once she got moving she would be all right.

CHAPTER FOUR

For several days Keith drifted along below the threshold of consciousness, mistily aware from time to time of people doing unspeakable things to him and of Molly's voice calling on him to awake. Out of habit, he resisted. He rallied briefly, aided by a doctor with a syringe, in order to mumble a brief but fairly coherent statement to a policeman who looked vaguely familiar.

Then he was away again into a world of dreams, some sick and some pleasantly erotic, to wake on what he learned was the fourth morning, limp as a wet cloth, still sleepy, ravenously hungry but allowed no more breakfast than he could take through a tube in his arm, and with no worse than a dull ache in his shoulder. When he moved, a bolt of rusty lightning skewered his shoulder and side.

If he was at a low physical ebb, at least his mind was sharp again. As soon as he woke he knew where he was. He had been a visitor to the hospital in Newton Lauder before, and a patient in it twice. Even, he thought, possibly in this very room. But not under the same doctor. The man who came to examine him was young, fit-looking in the way of young doctors, and a stranger; he appeared to have written his own name on his lapel-badge in a cultivated doctor's hand, totally illegible.

'I'm hungry,' was Keith's greeting.

The doctor nodded. 'Good sign.'

Keith supposed that it was reasonable to treat the statement as such. 'Please let me have something to eat,' he amended.

The doctor finished the preliminary phase of his examination and nodded again. 'Light diet from this evening,' he said to the accompanying sister – a hard-faced old prune, Keith thought – 'and he can come off the drip now.'

'I'd prefer a heavy diet, starting now.'

'You couldn't eat it. And if you did, you couldn't keep it down.' Which Keith admitted to himself was probably true.

The doctor started to unwrap Keith's shoulder.

'What the hell happened to me?' Keith asked. 'Was I shot?'

'The police will be asking you much the same question shortly. All I can tell you is that there was a phone call for an ambulance – anonymous, I believe. I'm told that they'd given up looking for you and written the call off as a hoax when an old spaniel joined them and started herding them up the hill like a couple of sheep. Anyway, you were brought in here, bleeding like a stuck pig and bound up, quite effectively, with some ripped-up pieces of ladies' intimate apparel. The theory has been voiced that you did the ripping-up and got skewered for your trouble. You had a short arrow sticking out of your shoulder, front and back, which your helpers

45

had very sensibly left in place.'

'Crossbow?' Keith asked.

'I wondered. But never having seen a crossbow arrow, bolt or – I believe I'm right? – quarrel, I'd no data to go on. The police have it now.'

'Only one with a square shaft is a quarrel,' Keith said.

The doctor finished his unwrapping and carefully peeled away the dressings. 'You seem to heal well. No sepsis.'

Keith turned his face away. The sight of his own damaged flesh was not for a totally empty stomach. 'When can I get out of here?'

The doctor delegated the rebandaging to the old prune and straightened up. 'God knows, we don't want to keep a precious bed occupied any longer than we have to,' he said. 'Do you have anyone to nurse you at home?'

'Yes.' Keith hoped that Molly would acquiesce.

'In that case, and if you keep up your progress, you might get home in about a week. But it'll be bed for you, or at least chair-bound convalescence, for another week. I'll want to take out the stitches a week from tomorrow, or you can get your own doctor to do it if you're at home.'

'What's the date?'

'Third of August, I think.' The doctor looked at his watch. 'Yes.'

'In nine days time,' Keith said, 'the grouse season opens.'

The doctor was inclined to be sympathetic. He did a little shooting when time permitted and he knew how much the opening day of the grouse

46

meant to a devotee. But facts were facts. 'It opens without you,' he said. 'Put it out of your mind. You seem to be very resilient to shock, but you lost a lot of blood.'

'I've been a donor around here for years. Now I'd like some of it back.'

'You've already had it back at an extortionate rate of interest. You were just about drained when they brought you in and still losing. And then we had to operate to close a damaged artery and repair some muscles. Apropos which, even if you're fit to stagger on to a moor on the twelfth, which I doubt, you wouldn't be able to stand the jolt of a gun on that shoulder.'

'I wouldn't feel the jolt from a four-ten.'

'I think you'd feel the thump of a fly landing on it,' the doctor said. 'And if you can hit grouse with a four-ten, you're a damn good shot.'

'I *am* a damn good shot,' Keith said.

'Well, you'll not be any damn good by the twelfth. Nor yet when duck and partridge come into season. Save yourself for the pheasants in October. Better still, wait until the hard weather pushes the geese on to Blatchford Loch.'

'I don't have permission for Blatchford Loch,' Keith said irritably. It was a sore point.

'I have. And if you've been a good boy I'll take you. A dawn flight,' the doctor said persuasively, 'and not too much walking. But if you don't believe me, ask sister for a mirror and take a good look at yourself. I won't wait. I hate to see a grown man cry.'

The prune-like sister departed in the wake of the

47

doctor, leaving Keith's rebandaging to a young nurse who giggled at everything he said. She fetched him a mirror and Keith inspected himself with a growing sense of horror. He had known that some day he would awake to find himself an old man with an old man's face, flesh wasted and jaw-line broken, and now it seemed that the day had come. Looking closely, he could see more silver hairs than usual in his black thatch. He lay back with a groan which sent the young nurse scurrying for the old prune.

When the peaceful boredom was at last broken, it was by the kind of ordered pandemonium which only an invaded hospital can produce. It began with a precautionary visit from the doctor. Then two policemen, stolidly pushing Keith and the furniture from place to place and back again, clearing a space along the wall of the small side-ward. Next came a file of half a dozen men, some embarrassed and some amused, all much of a height and colour, who shuffled into a line along the wall.

Through the middle of the line Chief Inspector Munro made his entrance, a tall, lean figure with a long and moody face. His uniform, as usual, was immaculate but slightly ill-fitting, as though no uniform could ever adapt itself to his Hebridean frame.

Keith and the chief inspector had developed, over the years, a relationship which vacillated between respect and revulsion, occasionally extending as far as a grudging affection. But this was Munro at his most official. 'It would not be reasonable,' he began in his careful West Highland speech, 'to ask whether you have seen any of these men before –'

'I've seen nearly all of them.'

'You will oblige me by not speaking just yet. I wish you to tell me whether the man who telephoned you and then met you is in the line-up.'

Keith was an experienced witness. He thought carefully. 'The man who met me is not in the line-up,' he said.

'You are sure?'

'Absolutely.'

Munro nodded. 'Very well. Clear the room.' He went out with the others and Keith could hear voices in the corridor. Munro returned, carrying a large, flat cardboard box and accompanied by a constable in uniform. Munro took the only chair, leaving the constable to perch uncomfortably on the windowsill and balance his notebook on his knee.

'You noticed the man second from the right?' Munro asked.

'The one who looked as if there was a nasty smell under what little nose he had? I noticed him. He was almost the only man present who I hadn't seen before – I've been breathalysed by more than one of them. He's a certain resemblance to his father.'

'Aye.' Munro looked gloomier than ever. 'That was Brian Batemore. You'll oblige me, in future, by naming the sons of less influential men. It is as well that this did not happen before the last election or after the next one.'

'Is Dad throwing his weight around?'

'Not yet, but it is probably only a matter of time.'

'I didn't accuse anybody,' Keith pointed out. 'I said that a voice on the phone claimed to be Brian Batemore, and that a man met me.'

Munro looked thoughtful. 'Did the man who met you have the same voice as the man on the telephone?'

'It seemed similar,' Keith said. 'He didn't say much after we met and you know how the telephone distorts a voice. I didn't notice any accent.'

'No accent?' Munro said sharply. 'You have surely not heard the real Brian Batemore. He has one of those Oxford accents and a haughty voice as if the Queen herself should take off her hat to him.'

'His father sounds the same. And he shouts.'

'So does this one. He has no alibi for the time when you were injured – but no more, I suppose, do a million others. He admits to knowing where the Foleyhill place is, and so do all the locals. Well, father or no father, we shall have to keep an eye on that young man. Now. . . .' Munro lifted the cardboard box on to Keith's feet and untied an encircling string. 'What do you make of this?'

'Crossbow,' Keith said. He studied the brass and aluminium weapon in Munro's hands. 'Barnett Commando. Two hundred and twenty pounds draw weight. Is that the bolt that hit me?' Keith took the short arrow into his left hand. 'Fifteen inch alloy hunting bolt with the broadhead tip. Bloody vicious. If I hadn't moved just as he fired, I wouldn't've stood an earthly.'

'The crossbow has your name on it,' Munro said.

'It has a little sticky label on it, of the kind we stick on all goods sold from my shop. We've never stocked that model. The label could have been transferred from a trout rod or a dog whistle. Where was the crossbow found?'

'About two hundred yards from where we found the deer's carcass and the stain of your blood. That would be beyond the range of the crossbow?'

'Well beyond its accurate range, but within its killing range.'

'You could not see the one place from the other for the foliage between.' Munro drummed his fingers on the lid of the box. 'Wait outside,' he said to the constable. But when they were alone he fell silent again.

'I know what you're going to say,' Keith said, 'so I'll say it for you. We've come to know each other over the years. There've been times I've maybe been up to a little something. There've been a damn sight more times you've *thought* I was up to something when I wasn't. And you want to know whether I'm up to something now.'

'Aye,' Munro said gratefully. 'That is just about it. Not that you'd be telling me.'

'Well, I'm not,' Keith said. 'I've no irons in the fire just now.'

'And you're not looking into something on be-half of somebody else?'

'No.'

'We shall no doubt be seeing in due course,' Munro said, 'as we've seen in the past. Do you think that you were lured up there in order to be killed?'

51

'No, I don't,' Keith said. 'Not by those two. I was still looking at the girl when I was hit—'

'I never doubted it,' Munro said.

'—and she was just as surprised as I was. I think that they lured me up there in order to frame me for a poaching charge. But why, I don't know. Once more, time may tell.'

'Very likely,' Munro said. Time, in the past, had often told him that Keith was holding back information for his own purposes. He looked ready to say more, but turned the subject. 'We most likely have a case of attempted murder,' he said. 'But we don't know for sure. If we treat the case as such they will no doubt put in somebody from C.I.D. in Edinburgh. If, for the moment, we treat it as a probable accident, we can keep it local. But it is a matter for yourself to decide. It is your neck that may be at risk.'

Keith quite understood. At that time, C.I.D. in Newton Lauder was kept at a lowly level, anything more serious than the theft of underwear from the washing lines resulting in an invasion of senior officers from Edinburgh, highly critical of the rural force and intolerant of local understandings.

'Let's call it an accident until you trace those two and find out what they have to say,' he suggested.

Munro departed soon thereafter. Keith felt guilty at withholding a wealth of information and conjecture; but if he had got his hands on something with an unseen value he wanted to be the first to know it.

CHAPTER FIVE

Unlike most prunes, the prune-like ward sister turned out to have a soft heart, susceptible to younger men with the dark good looks which Keith was fast recovering. She allowed him several dietary privileges and an occasional laughing cuddle at the bedside.

Despite these comforts Keith wanted to get home, and by dint of making himself thoroughly obnoxious and also of promising exemplary behaviour at home he secured his release on the fifth day of consciousness, to the tune of much head-shaking and many grim warnings.

He was wheelchaired to the car and sat with baby Deborah on his knee while Molly drove him home. Getting out of the car was a mighty effort and he tottered with swimming head, leaning heavily on Molly's shoulder, into the house and through to the kitchen where he flopped down thankfully into the basket-chair. The dogs pushed their heads at him in welcome.

'You're supposed to go to bed,' Molly said.

'And so I shall in due course. For the moment, I'm going to sit for an hour and then walk round the kitchen, and sit for another hour and walk round the house, and then sit for a third hour and walk round the garden.'

Molly raised her eyebrows but she knew better than to argue when Keith was in stubborn mood. 'I was just going to the shops when you phoned,' she said. 'I wasn't expecting you home for at least a week yet. There's nothing in the house but baby-food and those dried snacks we brought back from France.'

'I need feeding up,' Keith said. 'But start with a dried snack.'

'Read the instructions to me, then.'

Keith squinted at the tiny print. '*Videz le contenu*. . . . Dump the contents into a small casserole.'

'Got it. Keith, who'd do a thing like that to you, and why?'

'I don't know who, not yet. As to why . . . I'd have a bet that it's to do with those guns we bought in France. That makes sense of our car being gone through and Sir Henry Whatsit wanting to get an option on them. *Dosez le volume*. . . . Bung in a cupful of water.'

'Yes.' Without complying, Molly looked at him. Her clear, brown eyes were troubled. 'Keith, are you still in danger?'

'Shouldn't think so. What happened must have been an accident, or a stupid impulse, or a foul-up. I mean, even if the guns were a danger to somebody, or especially valuable to them, I can't see that anybody had anything to gain by knocking me off.'

'I can.'

'Why, then?'

54

Keith expected some reference to his capacity for making enemies. Molly surprised him. 'Suppose there was something wrong with one or more of those guns. Say they were stolen, or faked, or they'd been obtained by fraud or used in a murder or something. Somebody thinks he's got away with it. Then he finds out that you've bought them. What's next?'

'Eh? Oh. *Remuez bien.* Give it a stir. So I bought them. So what?'

'So this. Keith, how often have you given evidence in cases involving guns?'

'A dozen or more, I suppose.'

'And about antique guns?'

'Seven or eight.'

'Exactly,' Molly said. 'You've even been asked to investigate cases of fraud and things, and you've been consulted by the police. And anybody who knows you or reads your articles can see that you get *involved.* You never let go. You're the one person who'd be certain to spot whatever-it-is. What do I do next?'

'*Portez à ébullition.* Bring to the boil. Well, I haven't spotted whatever-it-is.'

'You will,' Molly said with quiet confidence. 'Keith, are you going to tell the police what you find out?'

'We'll decide that when we find out anything. Are you afraid?'

'Not for myself.' Molly stood beside him and ruffled his hair. 'I'll only be the poor little widow who puts them straight back on the market at a fat mark-up without noticing a damn thing. But,

Keith, are *you* safe?'

Keith ran his hand up and down her leg while he thought about it. It felt wonderful, but his body was in no condition to respond. 'Damned if I know,' he said at last. 'I'll take precautions. When you go shopping, call in on Janet and Wallace and find out whether they gave anybody our address in France. And I'll give you a note to pop through Ronnie's door.'

'And,' Molly said, 'I don't think you should go walking round the garden. Crossbows are too easily bought. It's boiling. What comes next?' She pulled reluctantly away from him.

'*Ajoutez une noix*. . . . Add a knob of butter. I've changed my mind. I won't go to bed, I'll potter about indoors until I get some strength back. There's one job I could do more or less one-handed, and that's to develop your holiday snaps if you do the loading into the spiral tanks for me.'

Molly nodded. The demands of the shop, the child and a husband in hospital had relegated photography to a low priority. It would mean taking Deborah along to the shops, but at least Keith would be kept safe and quiet. 'What comes next?' she asked.

'*Retirez du feu*. . . . Hell, I think it says something about a blue touchpaper,' Keith said. 'Where's the pocket dictionary?'

It was late afternoon before the warning note of the burglar-alarm told Keith of Molly's return. He heard the note stop as she punched the code to cancel the system and her cooing voice as she put

Deborah into her playpen. While the last prints were fixing he began, by the glow of the red safe-light, a conscience-stricken clean-up. Molly was fussy about her dark-room. By the time she tripped over the dogs which were waiting patiently on the landing outside the dark-room door, he had wiped up the worst of the spillages and restored some order. The working surface was clear except for a pair of antique pistols.

'Can I come in?' Molly's voice asked.

Keith opened the door and switched on the main light, blinking in the sudden glare. He was glad to take a seat again on the high stool.

'Sorry I've been so long,' Molly said. 'I chased Ronnie all over the town. In the end I had to put your note through his door just as you said, so I could have saved my time. Have you been working all afternoon?'

'I lay down for a bit while the negatives dried.'

'Wallace says that several people phoned to ask where we were. He and Janet just said "Near Riberac", and told them that letters would be forwarded and messages passed on.'

'That's what I thought.'

While she spoke, Molly was looking around. The negative strips were neatly racked, contact prints were pinned to the wall while overhead hung and fluttered many dozens of drying enlargements. She sidled along, studying the photographs. 'What *have* you been up to?' she demanded. 'Have you run me out of paper? I didn't think I even *had* this much.'

'I cut up some big sheets.'

'Do you know what that stuff costs? And I was taking photos of places. You've only printed cars. And why the pistols?'

'I didn't have anything more modern handy,' Keith said, 'just in case the wrong sort of person came to call. The way I see it, somebody was alerted that we'd bought something they wanted or feared – probably by that snippet in *The Scotsman*. So they found out that we were still in France and near Riberac. They didn't know that we were on a buying trip and shipping boxes of stuff home, so they decided to intercept our car. That meant picking us up around Riberac and following us home. Well, every time we parked, you hopped out and took photographs of the place. It would be interesting if the same car turned up too often, or if we could spot one which we'd seen on the road home. After all, if somebody was dropping hitch-hikers in front of us in the hope of our picking them up, he must have overtaken us several times.'

Molly nodded. There was usually some sort of method in Keith's frequent bouts of madness. 'And can you spot anything?'

'There must be a thousand cars in these photographs. And I'm tired. I think I'll go and lie down again until food's ready.'

'Good idea. Do you want a quick fry-up, or will you wait for a proper meal?'

'Both,' Keith said.

Keith slept that night like the dead, awoke feeling a little less like a wet flannel and ate most of a substantial breakfast.

Molly had set a card-table and chair outside the dining room french window, in a paved sun-trap sheltered by a jungle of overgrown rhododendron and azalea bushes. 'You need fresh air and sunshine,' she said. 'And if you keep the two dogs with you nobody can get near without you knowing.'

Keith settled down with the photographs, pen, paper, magnifier, radio and his two duelling pistols. Molly, ever the opportunist, brought out a rug, the playpen and Deborah. The dogs lay down, watching them both. Molly retired to her housework, secure in the knowledge that her charges were gathered together and safe under each others' supervision.

Ten minutes later her tranquillity was shattered by the sound of a shot.

A tray of dishes landed in the sink and Molly ran, heart in mouth, into the garden. At first glance all seemed safe. She leaned back against the jamb of the french window and held her heart.

To the evident delight of Deborah, Brutus, the young labrador, was presenting Keith with a bright bundle of feathers. 'I got that magpie that's been raiding other birds' nests,' Keith said happily. 'Would you fetch down my bag of loading gear?'

There was peace for an hour. Then the dogs stirred and looked towards the driveway. Keith could tell that the visitor was somebody known to them, but the dogs had met a thousand people on their forays with their master, not all of them

59

beyond suspicion. Keith raised one of his pistols. The large and rugged frame of Molly's brother came plodding round the corner of the house. Ronnie always looked to Keith as if he had been carved carelessly from the roots of a fallen oak.

He regarded Keith's pistols with amusement. 'You reckon to hit anything with those doodads?' As a stalker by profession, as well as a ghillie, Ronnie was inclined to despise anything smaller than his own favourite rifles.

'I just got a magpie,' Keith said.

'They're rifled, then?'

'Scratch-rifled.'

'Ah. Sir Peter's on the way. He's just having a crack with Molly. I'll away and fetch some chairs.' He disappeared towards the shed where the garden chairs were stored.

Keith made a few more left-handed notations, but he was smiling. Ronnie's employer, Sir Peter Hay, might be the biggest landowner thereabouts but he had been a good friend and patron to the Calders. Keith struggled to rise as the baronet's lanky form in its usual well-worn kilt came out through the french windows and Deborah, quick to recognize a plentiful source of sweets, held up chubby arms.

'Don't get up, my dear boy.' Sir Peter pushed him down with a fatherly hand on his shoulder and Keith felt the heat of a large cigar on his ear. 'I can see you're still weak as a kitten. I've been up north but Ronnie kept me posted. Got yourself shot, eh? Crossbow. Can't think of many husbands with one of those. Don't get on your high horse,' he added quickly. 'Only joking. I know you're a happily married man, now. You say so often enough. Molly was going to make coffee, but I said beer would do.'

'If you're smoking,' Keith said, 'take that cigar away from the playpen. I gave Deborah my powder-flask to chew on and she found out how to work the shutter. There's Black Silver gunpowder all over the rug and if anybody drops a spark she'll probably go up in a mushroom cloud.'

Sir Peter threw his cigar into the bushes and took one of the chairs which Ronnie had brought out. He lifted Deborah on to his knee, at the same time stooping to fuss with the dogs. 'I gather you owe your continued existence to this old beggar?'

'Not for the first time,' Keith admitted.

'Ronnie's big with tidings.'

Molly joined them with a tray and Ronnie contained himself while rings were pulled and glasses filled.

'Now,' Keith said.

'Aye.' Ronnie paused and took a pull at his glass. As Sir Peter's stalker he could read the writings of nature far more easily than he could a book. Verbalizing what he could read was more difficult. 'I went to Foleyhill and looked around, the way you asked. You'll mind that it was more than a week back, and very little soft ground. Mostly, all I could go by was faint tracks here and there. And where there was any kind of a path or a deer-track folk had mostly kept to it. There was once I found I was tracking myself.'

'If I'd thought it was going to be easy,' Keith

said, 'I wouldn't have had to bother with you.'

Ronnie took the flattery as no more than his due.

'M'hm. The ambulance-men had come and gone the same way and their track was clear. That took me to where Tanya had stopped and barked. They'd gone to her and she'd led them to where you were lying. From there, I picked up other tracks. There was a mannie who stalked and killed the roe, hung it in the tree and went off. I lost his track, but picked him up coming back again—I'm guessing it was the same lad. He'd settled himself down in bracken about fifty yards from the carcass and where he could see it. His bum-print was still clear to be seen.'

'And the other two?' Keith asked.

'That's not so easy. The police had been over the ground, and I couldn't separate his tracks and yours from theirs. But there was yin body that was lighter than the rest and with smaller feet. I'd guess that'd be the lassie. She'd just come up the once and hid herself behind a blackthorn. I lost her again after that.'

'Was there any sign that the man with the crossbow talked with anyone else?'

'I'd think not,' Ronnie said. 'I was wondering that myself. But if ever his tracks crossed with anyone else they just went straight past and no sign of either of them stopping, so I'd guess that they were made at different times.'

'That's small enough news to be big with,' Keith said.

'I'm not done yet. That was all I could see up there, and there was nothing dropped or left except blood and the deer's carcass. But I took a look at the face of the hill, and the other thing you asked, you were dead right. There was a line of fence-posts been set out up the hill, and the first half dozen had been let into the ground – not very cleverly, one was fallen down already.'

'Ah!' Molly said. 'So the man that fetched you up there, Keith, had something to do with the organization of the sanctuary. Is that it? Wouldn't they have known they were giving themselves away?'

'You never know how people's minds will work,' Keith said. 'I thought it was worth Ronnie's while having a look. I wanted to know whether somebody had picked on the place just because it's a lonely spot. But they knew so exactly the bait that I'd be bound to rise to. . . .'

'What comes next?' Molly asked. 'The police?'

Keith frowned. 'Not yet,' he said. 'I want to know a bit more before I give Munro anything to work on.'

'Just in case you can cut yourself in on something,' said Sir Peter.

'Maybe. I always like to know what I'm doing before I commit myself. So the first step is to find out who runs the sanctuary at Foleyhill.'

'You'll have your work cut out,' Sir Peter said bitterly. 'It adjoins my bit of moor and two of the farms on the other side are mine. What with roe-deer and rabbits coming over into the farmland and crows and foxes scouring the moor for grouse-chicks, I'm getting to detest the very sound of the name. So I've been trying to track down the . . . the sponsors, or whatever you call them.

'First of all, I thought that a wildlife sanctuary had to have some sort of official recognition, so I contacted the local authorities, who'd never even heard of it. I tried the R.S.P.B., who damned the operation as bringing their own reserves into disrepute by sheer bad management. Farquhar, the local kingpin of the Scottish Wildlife Trust, spoke his mind a bit more freely than I'd care to repeat. Nobody seemed to know who the hell, if anybody, was running the place, just reputedly "a bunch of students".

'Next, I looked into the ownership and found that the land belonged to Henry Batemore. I rang him up and he said that his stepson had begged the use of it for some organization he was connected with, and, since it was useless except for the few bits of forestry, he'd let them establish their sanctuary on it.'

'Stepson?' Keith said. 'Would that be Brian Batemore?'

'It would.'

'I thought he was the son. There's even a family resemblance.'

Sir Peter shook his head. 'Henry Batemore married late and for money, and from what I hear he got the worst of the bargain. The bride was some sort of a cousin of his, which might explain any resemblance. A widow with a ewe-lamb. I asked Batemore whether he'd sell me the land, and he said that he might but that he wouldn't want to commit himself until he'd spoken to his stepson, who'd just gone abroad again on holiday.'

How long ago was this?' Keith asked.

'Couple of days ago.'

'He was here last week. The bastard who enticed me up to Foleyhill used Brian Batemore's name, so the police lugged him into the hospital and set up an identity parade. I'd never seen him before that I could remember.'

'Well, he's gone again,' said Sir Peter. 'Farquhar said he thought the place was being run by some offshoot of the League Against Cruel Sports. Possibly a hunt saboteur's association, he guessed. Well, you don't find those people in the local phone book.' Sir Peter sighed deeply. 'Sign of the times. All of a piece with not wanting to do a decent day's work for a good day's pay. Class hatred and all that rot.'

'If you think about it, it was always predictable and it'll get worse,' Keith said. (Molly sighed and waited for a passage of home-spun philosophy. Keith could never recognize a trend without puzzling out an explanation to satisfy at least himself.) 'Look at it this way. This is an age of machinery and automation and microchips. In the developed world we can produce all the food and clothes and tellys we need without everyone slogging away for sixty hours a week as they used to. Even the forty hour week's too long. We're entering an age of leisure and nobody's teaching the poor little bastards to use it creatively. At the same time, people have drifted into the cities. And they can't drift back again easily. You can't even get planning permission to build a rural house any more, not unless you're a farmer.

'So you have people – students mostly, because they're at the age for radicalism – with loads of education, less knowledge, little understanding and bugger-all sense, wondering how to fill in their time

65

for the betterment of the world. God knows there's nothing much to do in a city,' Keith said with deep feeling. 'Only the best of 'em will find anything useful and creative to do. The rest'll march to ban this, or join the league against that, or decide to sabotage the other thing, because they have tiny minds and can only think negatively. Most of them will grow out of it.'

'They're a bloody nuisance until they do,' Sir Peter said. 'And I don't really believe that somebody shot you in defence of the birds that might otherwise be shot by you or your customers. What'll you do next?'

Keith pointed to the many little stacks of notes and photographs, weighted down against the fitful breeze by his two pistols, powder-flask and bullet-bag. 'I'm going to try to get a line on them through these. Nobody could follow as snap-happy a photographer as Molly around France without getting their car into a picture or two.'

'Good luck to you!' Sir Peter said. 'You'll not be fit to come out on the twelfth, I suppose?'

'I'll be there.'

'You can't shoot with your arm strapped up like that.'

'It won't be. I've another week to heal. And if I can't stand the kick of a twelve-bore I can bring something smaller. Or I'll pick up for you.'

Sir Peter looked doubtful but he was too polite to argue. 'I'll look forward to seeing you both, then,' he said. He kissed the top of Deborah's head and passed her to Molly. 'Time we were away, Ronnie. Again, Keith, don't get up. You'll need all your strength for the twelfth.'

Molly put Deborah back in her playpen and went to see the visitors off. She came back in a few minutes. 'I gave Ronnie his prunes-in-Armagnac,' she said. 'He borrowed some custard to go with them.'

Keith shuddered and went back to his photographs.

In mid-afternoon Keith appeared suddenly in the kitchen, a pistol in each hand. Molly squeaked and dropped a spoon. 'Wock –' She stopped and cleared her throat. 'What's happened?'

'Nothing.' Keith looked down at his pistols. 'You know what these are worth? I wasn't going to leave them in the garden.'

'You left Snookums in the garden.'

'With the dogs. They'll soon let us know if anybody comes near. Look.' Keith lifted his elbow and scattered photographs from under his arm on to the kitchen table. 'Could you pull these bits up bigger? The ones I've boxed in red? There's some paper left.'

Molly sighed. She flipped a photograph over. 'You didn't think to put the negative number on the back. And you've only printed the bits with cars in. How in hell do you expect me to find these fragments?'

'Do something clever,' Keith said hopefully.

'*You* do something clever. I've got dinner to cook.'

'I'll do that for you. You get enlargements sharper than I do.'

'That's because I don't clump around or play the radio while they're exposing.' Molly paused and balanced the pros against the cons. The desirability of Keith baby-sitting and of eating a meal that she had not had to cook for herself lost out against the tedium of searching the negatives for Keith's fragments and the stark horror of having to clean up the kitchen after him. 'I'll do dinner,' she said.

'Whatever you say.' Keith laid down one of his pistols and put an arm round Molly. They pressed together for a second and then parted. As he turned away Keith let himself frown. He enjoyed hugging his wife, but since his emergence from hospital he had felt no urge to make love. He carried his photographs up to the dark-room with a renewed determination to track down the man with the crossbow. The doctor had said that his impotence was the aftermath of shock and would soon clear up. But if the doctor was wrong, somebody was going to suffer.

By the afternoon of the following day, Keith had made his blow-ups and was back in the garden, complete with pistols, dogs and Deborah. His researches were almost complete when the dogs again gave warning of a visitor. This time it was Wallace's stringy form which arrived and flopped down into one of the garden chairs.

'How are you mending?' Wallace asked.

'Slowly. I wouldn't want to run a mile yet.' Keith was frowning.

'Don't worry, it may never happen.'

That was exactly what was worrying Keith. He stayed silent.

'You'll be f-fit for the twelfth?' Wallace asked.

'Come hell or high water.'

Molly, who had come to the french windows to investigate the sound of voices, made a derisory noise. 'If he's fit to do more than sit in a Land Rover,' she said, 'I'll believe in miracle healing.'

Keith had made up his mind that he could heal if he tried hard enough. He ignored her. 'All well at the shop?' he asked.

Wallace nodded. 'Well enough. The usual pre-season flurry. And I got rid of that Spanish gun you said nobody but a hairy idiot would buy.'

'Who bought it?'

'F-funnily enough, a hairy idiot. Keith, we've got a problem. With you being out of action, I've been turning away repair jobs. But while I was out of the shop, Minnie Pilrig went and accepted one from a man from Bonnyrig. He said he was taking his wife away for a few days' break, so we can't give it back. And Minnie says he was desperate to get the chequering re-cut and the barrels re-finished because he's got an invitation to Lord Moran's shoot on the twelfth and it's the only gun he ever hits anything with. Shall I run it into Edinburgh?'

'We can't afford to spend time and petrol sending business to our rivals,' Keith said. 'What make is it?'

'It says McSwale & Angus on the rib.'

'Nothing valuable, then. You've helped me blue enough barrels. Have a go. If you balls it up we can always do it again together.'

'I wouldn't trust myself to re-cut chequering,' Wallace said.

'You won't have to. I've never seen chequering worn away, except on a keeper's gun that was carried every day. It'll be bunged up with the snot and dandruff of a bygone age. Give it a good scrub with Janet's toothbrush.'

'All right,' Wallace said unhappily. 'I'll have a go. Are you any nearer to finding out who spiked you?'

Molly came away from the french windows and sat down. This was more important than shop-talk.

'I think so,' Keith said. He started to rearrange the enlargements. 'I've started from the assumption that somebody picked us up around Riberac, followed us and then dropped hitch-hikers in front of us at least once. And somebody else may have followed us all the way to the boat. I've been looking at the cars in Molly's photographs, and I spent yesterday evening dating them. I was looking for cars, preferably British, which don't show up until after that piece appeared in *The Scotsman*, and then show up in the right sort of places, and which I think I remember having seen on the way north.

'Now, here's a bit of a shot of the square at Riberac when we went to the market there. It's taken from about outside that café with the crash loo, Molly. See the red outline on it? Here's a pull-up of that bit.'

Molly took the second enlargement out of his hand. 'That's fine-grain film,' she said, 'and you've pulled it up until the grain looks like BB shot, but it's as sharp as a needle. Shows what a steady hand I've got.'

'And I wasn't clumping around in the dark-room. Didn't have the strength. See that car there?'

70

Molly looked where his pencil was pointing. 'The Capri?'

'Right. Now, while we were on the road home, somewhere before Angoulême, I remember seeing a shit-coloured Capri in the mirror—'

'*What* colour?'

'—a brown Capri, with one of those green plastic strips over the windscreen. You know what I mean, they say "Charles and Diana", or whatever. I was reading it backwards just before it overtook us, but it caught my attention. It said "Engaged" over the driver and "Vacant" in front of the passenger's seat.'

'He'd be a bloody fool to leave that on.'

'That's what I thought,' Keith said. 'He probably took off his spotlamps and dangling dollies which might have helped to make the car memorable, but he'd been looking at the sunstrip so long he'd stopped seeing it.'

Molly was busy with the magnifier. 'I think it says what you said, but it's right at the limit of definition and you can't make out the number. Without any colour. . . .'

'In a way,' Keith said, 'it helps having them in black-and-white. Look at this one. We stopped in Verteillac on the way back and you took this shot from outside the Crédit Agricole while I was cashing a cheque inside.'

Molly studied the new photograph under the magnifier while Wallace tried to peer over her shoulder. 'It could be the same car,' she said, 'but you can only see the last two letters on the sun-thing.'

'But it ends in N.T. How many names can you think of?'

'Charley and Aunt,' said Wallace.

'That's about all. And the number-plate's clear and sharp.'

'You're only guessing that it's the same car,' Molly said.

'I would be,' Keith said. 'But did you notice the girl standing beside the tree?'

'I didn't,' Molly said, 'but you'd be bound to.'

'Remember our hitch-hiker? That's why I said that the lack of colour might be a blessing. She was blonde when we picked her up. The girl with the camera up at Foleyhill was red-haired. The day we got back here, I was doing some shopping. A red-haired girl looked into the shop window, and later a brunette drove past in a brown Capri. I think they were all one and the same lassie. She could have had several different colours of those nylon wigs, and if she swapped them around and changed her sunglasses now and again who'd recognize her? A girl with long hair, the hair-colour's the first thing you notice.'

'Second,' Molly said.

'True. But when you've seen one–two, I mean–you've seen them all. Then you get around to the face later on.'

Molly was scowling through the magnifier. 'It could be her.'

'Now.' Keith changed photographs again. 'This is from a different frame, same place, same time, adjacent on the film. See the lad by the phone-box? It looks like the man who met me and took me up Foleyhill. I ought to be sure, but I'm not. I hardly looked at his face, he'd got me too interested in looking around.'

'Keith,' Molly said sharply. 'Do you remember? After we'd picked up the girl –?'

'The hitch-hiker? The second one, who turned away about when he could see that the girl was in our car? I was wondering about that.'

Wallace removed the photographs and the magnifier from Molly's determined grasp. 'If there were two hitch-hikers there must have been a driver as well,' he said.

'But we didn't see him.'

'Perhaps you didn't, but I may've seen him. And,' Wallace said suddenly, 'I think I d-did.' He laid his finger on the first photograph. A round-faced young man, in jeans and a T-shirt which proclaimed that he had undergone a vasectomy, was buying a loaf off a market stall. Either he was below average size or the lady in charge of the stall was enormous – possibly, Keith thought, both. 'That lad, or one damn like him, was in the shop and asking where you two had gone. And this other lad, the one you say may have been a hitch-hiker and may have taken you up to Foleyhill. . . . Keith, you remember the day you got back. We were talking in the shop, and a man came in and looked at trout rods. You had your back to him most of the time, but I saw his face. That's him.'

'And I was in the process of telling you that all the guns were coming over by coaster,' Keith said bitterly. 'I didn't name the boat, did I?'

'Not that I remember. I wonder whether these are all the same bunch,' Wallace said. 'If your car was done twice there must've been two different lots. Wouldn't they have bumped into each other?'

'Possibly,' said Keith. 'But we don't know that they both got to Riberac at the same time. I mind that we had the timetable of the Dieppe sailings lying around on the back seat for a while. Anybody who saw that might have waited for us at Dieppe.'

They shuffled the stacks of photographs. Molly picked up another shot of Riberac, taken a few days before the others. 'There's a dark Jag. . . . This was the day we lunched at the Chêne Vert, and it's parked further up the same street as if the driver's watching for us coming out of the hotel. There was a dark blue Jag. of the same model – well, it looked the same to me – a few cars behind us in the queue for the boat at Dieppe.'

They puzzled over the photographs, but without extracting any more information from them, until Wallace said that he had to go. Molly elected to walk with Wallace to his car. From the corner of the house they looked back to the sun-trap, where Keith was either deep in thought or falling asleep. His hand dangled in the playpen and Deborah was earnestly counting his fingers, watched by the jealous young labrador and the complacent old spaniel. Wallace sighed. He and Janet yearned for a child of their own, so far without success although, as Janet said, it was fun trying. 'It must be wonderful to have a bairn,' Wallace said.

'It used to be,' Molly said. 'Having two of them can get a bit much at times.'

Wallace nodded. He knew exactly what she meant.

CHAPTER SIX

Keith came partially out of his reverie. Leaving Deborah and the dogs to their own devices, he made his way to his study and phoned the police. Sergeant Ritchie was on duty and came to the phone.

'Dougie?' Keith said. 'Keith Calder here. I want a favour. Would you rather call me back?'

'Aye. I'll do that.'

A few minutes later the phone rang and Keith heard the succession of rapid pips which denotes a coin-box. 'What favour?' Ritchie's voice asked.

'First off,' Keith said, 'I want to trace an owner from a car number.'

'I couldn't be doing a thing like that,' Ritchie said. 'It wouldn't do at all. These things are terrible confidential and private.' There was silence for a few seconds. 'How would you like to see over the new building?' he asked.

'I'd be very interested,' Keith said.

'Quarter to twelve the morn, be in the square near your shop.'

'Right,' Keith said. He broke the connection and dialled again. He wanted Ronnie's services as chauffeur.

Ten minutes before noon the next day, Sergeant Ritchie's rosy face appeared at the door of Ronnie's Land Rover. He opened the door and climbed up, puffing gently because his initially broad form had been spreading over the years. Keith humped himself painfully on to the middle seat.

'Up towards your cottage, Ronnie,' Ritchie said. 'But keep going right-handed.' He guided them on to new tarmac and round the bulk of the new police building. Scaffolding was being dismantled, and painters were cleaning the warning labels off the windows. They parked between contractors' vehicles.

'Come when I give you a wave,' Ritchie said. He fumbled for the latch, clambered out and trudged across the tarmac to a side-door. A younger constable came out and hurried off. Ritchie waved and they walked over to join him.

'I'm relieving him while he gets his dinner,' Ritchie said. 'This way I can show you around, and nobody the wiser. The thing is, the builders are supposed to be finished but they've gone late. And there were sub-contracts that couldn't be stopped and deliveries that had to be made. Like the new terminals to the Police National Computer.'

'That's what you're guarding?' Keith asked.

Ritchie shook his head. 'Who'd want to steal that sort of thing? It's the booze, man. This bit here, the staff club, came into use last week. And all the champagne for the open ceremony turned up. And with the place empty but for the builder lads. . . .'

'That figures. I never tasted champagne,' Ronnie said.

77

'You're not tasting it now,' Ritchie said. He led them into a large room. One end was fitted out as a bar. 'You called at just the right time or I couldn't have helped you. There's a purge on about unauthorized access to the computer. Seems one of the highheidyins did a spot-check. He wondered why one of the stations in the city had called up a list of all the local tarts. The station syndicate had just had a win on the pools, and it turned out that they were having a celebration stag party. Now the tapes for every day are collected for checking, and the Lord help you if you've no good reason for the questions you've asked the computer.'

'Well, then –'

'But the new gear, the terminals in this building, they're in and working but there's nobody to see what gets wiped off the recording tapes. Come through this way.'

'Somebody should stay here on guard,' Ronnie said. 'I'll do it.'

'Oh no you don't,' Ritchie said firmly. 'You just come along with me.'

'He's used those words before,' Keith said.

Ritchie unbolted a pair of doors and led them into an internal corridor which, unlike the clubroom, was functionally decorated and still showed signs of missing finishes. Near to the front of the building he turned into a severe-looking office equipped with four computer consoles, a supervisor's desk with monitors, automatic wall-displays and all the paraphernalia of space-age police work. He threw some switches at the supervisor's desk and took his seat at a console. 'What do you want to know?' he asked.

'Fawn Capri,' Keith said. He put down a slip of paper beside Ritchie. 'This number. Who owns it?'

'No problem.' Keith watched carefully as Ritchie keyed the console. 'Valerie Duguidson, Hawthorns, Bonnyrigg.'

'Miss or Mrs?'

'Miss. Could she have married since the last time she taxed her car?'

'For all I'd know,' Keith said. He remembered that there had been a slight facial resemblance between the girl and the young man who had met him at Foleyhill. 'Does she have a brother?'

'Ring her up and ask her. There's no way I can tell from here.'

'You can call up things like criminal records and firearms certificates, can't you?'

'I wouldn't know his name.'

'Duguidson's an uncommon name. Call them all up.'

Ritchie thought about it. 'I could,' he said. 'But you two stand well back. Some of this is gey confidential.' When Ronnie and Keith were well out of range he keyed the console again. 'Two Duguidsons,' he said. 'One of them lives over in the west and does credit card frauds, but the other . . . you've hit it. Hugh Duguidson, same address as the lassie. Nothing serious. He swatted one of our men with a placard during a demo at Torness and then got himself in contempt of court. That all you want?'

'What else can you find out?'

Ritchie began keying in to different programs. 'Neither of them wanted . . . not disqualified drivers . . . no shotgun or firearms certificates . . . no

79

licence to keep explosives . . . no . . . that's about the lot.'

'Brian Batemore,' Keith said. 'What kind of car does he have?'

'Yon lad that was up at the hospital because somebody used his name? Come on, now, Keith. That's the Shadow Home Secretary's son.'

'Stepson.'

'After the next election, his dad could be my boss's boss's boss's boss.'

'For God's sake,' Keith said, 'You're Scottish Office, not Home Office. I'm not asking for anything confidential. He drives around in it.' Behind Ritchie's back, he made a face at Ronnie.

'Anyway,' Ritchie said, 'it doesn't work that way round. Give it a number and it'll tell you who owns the car. But you can't just put in the owner's name.' He fumbled through a typed booklet. 'I don't think so,' he added uncertainly.

'Try it,' Keith suggested.

'No, I'm trying no experimentation with this thing. I might wipe its memory out, and then think what a stishie there'd be.'

Keith could think of more than one acquaintance who would be glad if that were to happen. He leaned over Ritchie's shoulder. 'Just out of interest,' he said, 'just a hypothetical question. If you wanted to wipe the memory clean, how would you set about it?'

'You'd do it too, you bleeder.' Ritchie suddenly noticed Ronnie's absence. 'Where's he gone?'

'I think he wandered back-the-way.'

Ritchie took off like a lurcher going after a hare.

Keith settled himself at the console. He was no expert on computers, but it was his experience, gained from the mini-computer and the word processor that he and Wallace used for the business, that many computers could perform functions which the original programmer had never dreamed of. He had watched Ritchie with care and had digested the salient part of the procedures over Ritchie's shoulder from the instruction-book. There was nothing abstruse about them. The methodology was clear-cut. Starting from the question, 'How would I wish to be addressed if I were a computer?' Keith began keying in. The computer responded with dumb insolence, or by flashing up such comments as 'Error' or 'Insufficient data' on its screen.

Ritchie was battering at the door of the clubroom. 'Come out, you diffy gowk,' he roared. 'By God, Fiddler, I'll lib you with a rusty gullie when I catch hold of you.' And more, much more, to similar effect.

Keith must have found an acceptable formula. Honour satisfied, the computer suddenly relented and began on a list of car-owning Batemores. Keith watched in fascination.

Ronnie had departed, without, in fact, broaching any of the bottles. Keith and Sergeant Ritchie were left to make their way out through the builders' workings. Keith pacified Ritchie at last and walked down to the square. He was very tired and the sight of the Land Rover waiting outside the shop was tempting, but he made his way inside.

Wallace was alone in the shop, patiently re-arranging stock in preparation for the next rush of customers. He fetched a chair for Keith. 'Minnie didn't recognize anybody in the photographs,' he said.

'I didn't suppose she would. She never looks at faces. Anyway, our label was probably transferred from somebody's discarded carton. Wal, did you say that we had a customer in Bonnyrigg?'

Wallace nodded. 'The man with the McSwale & Angus twelve-bore. You were right about the snot and dandruff. The chequering came up sharp and clean. But now the wood's a paler colour than the rest.'

'You've scrubbed away the patina from ump-teen years of shitty fingers,' Keith said. He took a moment for thought. Wallace was not up to tricky work with leather dyes. 'Darken it with shoe polish. Then, when it's dry, wax the whole stock. If he notices any difference, tell him to bring it in to me when I'm better. Have you done the blueing?'

'Not yet. I'm just finishing the cleaning off.'

'Careful of fingerprints. Wal, I want some gossip from Bonnyrigg. Ring up, see if you can get him to collect the gun from me at Briesland House. Better still, time it so that his wife comes for it. Wives notice the kind of thing I want to know.'

'Will do,' Wallace said. 'Now, Keith, there are one or two bits of business. . . .'

Keith yawned in his face. 'Sorry, Wal, I'm too tired. Think I'll get Ronnie to run me home now.'

Keith spent an hour with the French photographs and then, tired from his expedition, took to his bed and slept through until the dawn. To Molly's surprise he seemed to have lost interest in the mystery and next morning was back at work on his catalogue, typing clumsily, left-handed, at the word processor. When Molly was out of sight he exercised his right arm. It hurt like hell, but he thought that his use of it was improving. The Glorious Twelfth was now only four days off.

On the far from glorious tenth – the weather had turned to cold and drizzle – Keith was at work when Molly appeared beside him. 'There's a lady come to see you,' she said.

'And very welcome you are, too,' Keith retorted. He ran his hand up the inside of her leg.

Molly pretended not to notice. 'Not me,' she said. 'A Mrs Threadgold.'

'Tell her –' Keith paused. 'Threadgold? The lady from Bonnyrigg?'

'Yes.'

'Fetch her in.'

Keith covered the word processor and moved to his desk. He thought about his wife. Molly had been wearing stockings. She was used to the warmth and comfort of tights but admitted that they lacked glamour. So when she wore stockings they were for her husband's benefit. What worried Keith was that the benefit seemed to be unobtainable.

He wiped the frown off his face as Mrs Threadgold entered – a slim, bird-like lady in her forties or fifties, wearing a blouse and skirt in trendy colours. 'You have my husband's gun ready?'

'Do sit down. I don't know if my partner's finished it yet.'

'Wallace left a gun here a few minutes ago,' Molly said. 'He asked me to show it to you. He's coming back to speak to you after he's done another errand. I'll get it.' She brought in a leather leg-of-mutton case. It had Mr Threadgold's name on a label.

'This is it, then.' Keith started to unbuckle the case. 'You'll want to see it?'

'Bless you, no!' Mrs Threadgold said, smiling. 'I wouldn't know t'other from which. I'll just take it along. How much is it?'

'I won't know until I see my partner. Never mind. I'll send in a bill. But don't run along yet,' Keith said quickly. 'I wanted to ask you about Bonnyrigg. Have you lived there long?'

Mrs Threadgold smiled again. She had a nice smile. 'Twenty-two years. All my married life.'

'Do you know a house called Hawthorns?'

The smile snapped off. 'Hawthorns? My dear, I could talk for hours.'

'Then we'll be needing a cup of coffee to see us through.' Keith looked up at Molly, who had waited by the door.

Molly hesitated. She knew that if she left the room for as long as it took to make coffee she might never catch up with the discussion. 'Let's all go through to the kitchen,' she suggested.

'Lovely!' Mrs Threadgold prattled on as she fluttered after Molly. 'I seem to have been driving all day and I'm parched. Bill won't be back until next week, and I'm doing errands for him all over Scotland. What a pretty kitchen!' she added.

Keith was quite prepared for interminable female chatter, but only on subjects chosen by himself. 'Do sit down and tell us all about Hawthorns,' he said. 'Who lives there?'

Mrs Threadgold settled herself comfortably and placed her handbag neatly on the table. 'It used to belong to a Miss Nettley. Such a charming old lady. We knew her well. Our garden, you see, backs on to the Hawthorns. Miss Nettley was what I suppose you'd call a good neighbour. Hawthorns' garden must be quite half an acre but it was always perfect, and there was never any fuss even when the children kicked a ball over. But then she died – cancer, poor thing! – and she left the house to her niece, a young person called Duguidson.'

Keith had brought with him his packet of photographs. He drew out the enlargement showing the girl in Verteillac. 'Is this her?'

'That's the girl. A flighty creature and a terrible neighbour. But, to be fair, I met her mother once, a real dragon, and I suppose the poor girl was desperate to get away from home. Being left Hawthorns must have seemed a godsend. But she couldn't keep up a house that size on a student grant, so she and her brother opened the place up to fellow students. We're handy to Edinburgh, you see.'

Keith produced the photograph of the young man beside the telephone-box. 'Is this the brother?'

Mrs Threadgold only had to make a quick glance. She nodded. 'I think his name's Hugh. Well, they started off running a sort of co-operative hostel, but the inevitable happened. I mean, the most orderly students go into halls of residence or digs found by the university. The outcasts ended up in Haw-thorns and it degenerated into a sort of commune. The house is becoming a slum and the garden's gone to pot – quite literally, I mean, old cars parked where the lawn used to be, and I think the only thing cultivated is cannabis.' Mrs Threadgold looked shocked and yet she twinkled slightly at her little pun.

Molly paused in the act of pouring. 'Any particular sort of outcasts?' she asked.

Keith knew that he could trust Molly to extract every ounce of human gossip. He left them to it for a minute while he fetched a copy of a motoring magazine. Mrs Threadgold was in full flood when he returned. 'Not exactly hippies, nor punks, nor skinheads either,' she was saying. 'You see the occasional caftan or headband, and the men mostly look rather biblical. There's one they call Creepy Jesus who I'd hate to meet on a dark night or in a lonely place. But in the main they're reasonably clean, but intense.'

Molly made an enquiring noise. Mrs Threadgold took it to refer to the cream. 'I won't, thank you. My daughter says that if I don't watch my figure nobody else will. Well, I'm past all that sort of thing, but there's no point letting yourself go, is there?

'What I was saying probably didn't sound as if there was very much wrong with them, but it's their *manner*. Arrogant. They seem to think that they know it all and they despise the rest of us and what we do and stand for. They ask the library for cranky books on organic diet and existentialism and

Christian Science, and then act as if the girl's incompetent because she doesn't have them ready to hand. And woe betide you if you stand in their road. Some of them would walk right over you.'

'They sound as if they'd be anti-bloodsports,' Molly suggested.

Mrs Threadgold's eyebrows shot up. 'They're anti-everything else. I never thought of it before but it would explain a lot. They know my husband shoots. They could hardly not, with him standing on the lawn most mornings, practising what he calls 'dry mounting' and frightening the cats. It would explain why they've taken such a spite at us. We have to lock the car in the garage overnight or the tyres are flat in the morning and worse. And we had to give up keeping hens because they just disappeared. And, my dear, the graffiti! We've called the police time and again. They found feathers in the Hawthorns dustbin, but there was nothing to show that they came from our hens. And then, would you believe, they had the gall to ask Bill for a legal opinion. Something about inheritance. I hoped it might get them away, but Bill said there was nothing in it.'

'It's beastly when you can't trust your neighbours,' Molly said.

Keith, who never trusted any neighbour, broke in quickly. 'Have you ever seen a dark blue Jaguar there?'

Mrs Threadgold thought about it but shook her head. 'We hardly ever see the front of the house. It's in a different street, one that we never go down.'

'How about a red Morgan?'

'One of those little three-wheelers with the engine out in front?'

Keith put down the motoring magazine in front of her. 'One like this,' he said.

'Now I've given my age away, haven't I? Yes, a red car something like that parks round the back from time to time. Overnight, usually. And about a month ago it was there for a full week with one wing all crumpled.'

By the time the coffee was finished they had filled in the details but without learning any more of significance. Mrs Threadgold said her thank-yous and got up.

'You've been very helpful,' Keith said. 'I can phone you if I think of any more questions?'

'Yes, of course.' She headed for the front door and her car.

'And you'd better take the gun along.'

Mrs Threadgold could hardly have been a mile on her way when Wallace put his head round the kitchen door. 'Is there any coffee left?'

'Mrs Threadgold finished the pot,' Molly said. 'I'll put some more on.'

'Don't bother. She's been, then?'

'Took the gun away a few minutes ago,' Keith said.

Wallace sat down as if his knees had given way. 'She t-took it? I only b-brought it to show you. What did you think?'

'Didn't see it,' Keith said. 'What was wrong? Fingerprints showing up silver in the blueing?'

'The – er – colour of the barrels came out . . . sort of different.'

'Don't look so worried. It happens to all of us. If the blue had a greenish tinge, that was because you contaminated the blueing solution with neutralizing agent.'

Wallace swallowed audibly. 'Pink,' he said at last.

Keith's imagination refused to recognize the concept. 'If there's a reddish tinge,' he said, 'you had it too hot.'

'P-pink,' Wallace said desperately. 'The exact, self-same pink of a new pair of cheap corsets.'

Keith sat with his mouth open. Molly set the percolator to work again. It was going to be needed. 'Couldn't you have rubbed it off and started again?' she asked.

'I tried that. The finish is as hard as steel, much harder than blueing. And with a lovely polish. I could never have got it off without wrecking the gun. I brought it round to get Keith's advice.'

Keith had been turning over his past experiences and his recollections of elementary chemistry and he had come up with one possible answer. 'What I think you must've done,' he said, 'was to use the browning solution I keep for antique guns and then used the neutralizing agent for a blue finish.'

'Never mind what I must have done,' Wallace said. 'What are we going to do? We can't have him turning up at Lord Whatsit's shoot with pink barrels. He'll never live it down.'

'You could chase after her,' Keith suggested, 'and lend him another gun.'

'That's the only one that he hits anything with.'

'Get the damn thing back,' Keith said, 'and we'll re-do it together.'

'You can't,' Molly said. 'She was driving straight off to join her husband somewhere up north. They're not coming back until after the twelfth.'

There was a depressed silence.

'I suppose she didn't say where they were going to be?' Wallace asked.

Molly shook her head.

Keith was beginning to see the funny side. 'You said the gun was a McSwale & Angus?'

'Yes.'

'When he rings up –'

'And will!'

'– to complain –'

'That's for sure!'

'– tell him that Jock McSwale spent a lifetime trying to perfect a finish the exact colour of August heather, but that's as near as he could get.'

Wallace brightened up. 'Did he really?'

'I shouldn't think so. McSwale & Angus were ironmongers, somewhere around Buchanan Street. They used to buy guns by the hundred from the Birmingham trade, with their own name on them. They went bust some time during the reign of Edward the Seventh.'

CHAPTER SEVEN

Two cars and a Range Rover were halted where the first stretch of track dipped down to the gulley cut by a small burn. Ronnie stopped his Land Rover and climbed down. Keith and Molly followed.

The twelfth had dawned colder and a stiff breeze was ruffling Sir Peter Hay's grey locks. He was engaged in anxious discussion with Hamish, his part-time keeper – a large and silent man, Hamish, who spoke rarely although his beard spoke volumes for him. It was speaking now, in furious twitches, of ruin and damnation.

'Don't blame yourself,' Sir Peter was saying. 'It's my fault you weren't up here. But if we'd known a couple of days ago I could have got the Argocat down from up north and let those idle Yanks make do with a Land Rover and Shanks' pony.'

'Trouble?' Keith asked.

'Look for yourself. There's no way to get a vehicle over the burn.'

They looked down. The wooden bridge over the burn had been destroyed. A fire had been lit

91

in the bed of the stream, dry after the fine spell. The embers were still smoking.

'Kids?' Keith said. 'Or tinkies? Or deliberate vandals?'

'Who knows? The devil of it is,' said Sir Peter, 'that in this wind we'll have to start from the far end. Are you fit to hoof it that far?'

Keith understood. Grouse can only be driven upwind when they are going home. 'If needs must,' he said. 'But I'll not be quick. I'll set off now, and the others can overtake me.'

'All right.' Sir Peter scratched the back of his neck. He looked more harassed than Keith could remember seeing him. 'I've got a meal for twenty packed in the back of the Range Rover and it'll have to be humped to the top barn. And you won't be fit to carry anything extra.'

'I'm afraid not,' Keith said. 'I can just about manage my gun, game bag and cartridges.'

'How about one of these?' Sir Peter handed Keith a lightweight transmitter-receiver. He had recently equipped the workers on his various estates with radios, primarily so that the equipment would be available for the control of large shooting parties.

Keith slipped it into his pocket. 'I'll leave Brutus with you,' he told Molly. 'I'll take the old 'un. She's just about as knackered as I am, so we'll do well together.'

Molly put on her patient face. 'If I've got to help carry the lunch,' she said, 'you could at least take this for me.' She hung a camera around Keith's neck.

'I'll get moving,' Keith said, 'before anybody thinks of anything else to hang on me. See you later.'

He set off. His gun felt unfamiliar under his left arm but hurt him if he shifted it to his right. The old spaniel frisked carefully over the heather. He called her to heel in case she disturbed the birds, although much of the heather on this part of the moor was too short for a good population of grouse. Sir Peter Hay was a thrifty landlord, indulging the estates rather than himself or his guests. The best pheasant-shoots on his land were all profitably let and the revenue ploughed back into machinery, land reclamation and afforestation, Sir Peter retaining for himself only a place in a syndicate on a modest shoot. With the stretches of moor in his ownership Sir Peter was equally frugal, keeping for himself a moor which was so heavily predated from Foleyhill that it could make no economic sense if kept for grouse alone. The red grouse shared their habitat with black-faced sheep. The heather was religiously burned for grouse, which suited the sheep very well. But the sheep cropped the heather short, which suited the grouse very little. So Keith was not expecting much of a bag that day. But still, it made an enjoyable social outing to open the season. Sir Peter made up for the paucity of game by providing a sybaritic lunch. No beaters were hired, the beating being done by the guns who took turns to form a walking party. First time over, before the birds had learned caution, walking guns might get their share of the sport.

93

Keith came out of his reverie. He spared a smile for the thought of Mr Threadgold uncovering his gun, perhaps for the first time, on Lord Moran's more prestigious moor. But his smile was fleeting.

His route climbed gently for a quarter of a mile, then crossed a stretch of level moor and dropped into the valley beyond. From the crest Keith could see the barn beckoning across the valley. It looked a thousand miles away. His legs were trembling. The gun began to weigh a ton, Molly's camera a hundredweight.

He took it slowly down the hill. The rough surface was harder going than pavement or lawn, the short heather slightly better. From time to time his fellow guests, old friends mostly, strode past with insulting ease carrying great burdens of lunch and gear. Keith exchanged greetings with them and tried to look as if he could keep up if he wanted to.

By the time he reached the valley's bottom Keith's strength was gone. He lowered himself cautiously on to a rounded boulder. He could easily have fallen asleep except that the breeze came buffeting up the valley, bringing a chill foretaste of winter to come.

The next man down the hill was his brother-in-law, hugging a carton of bottles and with his gun slung in its sleeve over his shoulder. He seemed glad to set down the carton for a minute and to rest his broad rump on it. 'You look knackered,' he said.

'I should do, because I am.'

'I told you you would be.'

'Everybody told me,' Keith admitted. 'Well, it was worth a try but I'll have to give up. I'll never make it up that hill.' He waited for some caustic remark in reply.

'M'hm. Well, if you're not fit to go on you'll not make it back the way you came, that's just as steep.' Ronnie scratched his head. 'I'll tell you what. You follow the valley down-the-way. There's no climbing at all. It brings you out at the old quarry at Foleyhill. I'll bring the Land Rover round and pick you up later.'

Keith thought it over. A mile or two downhill he could manage. 'Thanks,' he said. 'I'll do that. Make my apologies to your esteemed boss.'

'Make them yourself. He'll be down in a minute or two.'

'No, I won't hang about,' Keith said. 'This wind's cutting me in half. You'd better give Peter his gadget back.'

'Keep the wee radio,' Ronnie said. 'You can use it to tell me whether the track's clear all the way down. If it is, I'll fetch the Land Rover round at lunchtime and bring you right up to the barn.'

Keith watched Ronnie's departing back with some amazement. Two original thoughts in quick succession demanded a permanent memorial. He would have to come back some day and carve an inscription on his boulder.

He began to plod gently down the bottom of the valley, nursing his strength. He passed the end of the long tract of coniferous plantation which marked the boundary between Sir Peter's moor and the policies of Foleyhill. Here the valley

95

broadened and the wind, less confined, was gentler. He was glad to sit down again on a grassy bank. After a minute's rest he took the radio out of his pocket.

The first voice to come through was Molly's. 'Keith, are you listening? Are you all right? Over.'

Keith assured Molly of his continued survival and relative health. When he released the 'Transmit' button, Hamish's voice took over.

'Sir Peter, some daft bugger's vandalized the butts. They're just not usable at all.'

Sir Peter's voice came over, irritated but decisive. 'The standing guns will have to fall back on the edge of the wood and the beginning of the gulley.'

Keith progressed further down the valley and rested again. The radio kept him abreast of developments while the standing guns were moved and the walkers briefed and drawn into line. He knew the ground well and could follow their progress in his mind, aided by the radio and by an occasional shot. Despite the irritating vandalism it was shaping up to be a good day, and he promised himself some blistering revenge on whoever had made the hole in his shoulder. But his route seemed clear enough to take Ronnie's Land Rover. Perhaps he could still attend lunch and join in the afternoon's sport, if his knees would stop shaking.

The walking party had, in Keith's judgement, covered only a third of the first drive – they would be near the old sheep-pen – when a new voice came on the air, that of a young doctor who,

Keith knew, was walking at the boundary end of the line. 'There's a dog hassling the sheep, driving them across our path. Big black and white collie. It behaves like a trained dog, I think it's being worked by somebody inside the fir trees beyond the boundary using a silent whistle. What'll we do? The sheep will be pushing the grouse ahead of them. Over.'

'Just carry on,' came Sir Peter's calm voice. 'The birds should be used to Dougall's dog moving sheep. Who's got the radio at the bottom end of the standing line? Jack Frazer? Over.'

'Aye, Sir Peter.'

'Jack. You and Molly pull round the bend of the gulley. If any birds get up in front of the sheep they'll swing downhill and go over you.'

Keith got to his feet and lurched on, turning this new development over in his mind. Occasional single shots, as the walking guns took their chances with rising birds, gave way to a brief crackle as a covey went over the standing guns. The old spaniel came close to Keith for reassurance. She had never known her master walk away from the shooting before. Silence fell again.

Keith's legs were turning into jelly and a great lethargy was creeping over him. He stumbled through a gateway and found a seat with his back to the dry-stone wall, out of the wind and with the sun on his face.

The radio clicked and hissed. 'Seven and a half brace,' said Sir Peter's voice. 'Not a bad start.'

It was almost too much trouble, but Keith drew out the radio and pressed the 'Transmit' button. 'I must have heard fifty shots,' he said. 'That's not even one for three. Over.'

'I don't think we fired fifty,' Sir Peter said mildly, 'and with this wind behind them they're flying as if they had after-burners.'

Hamish's voice broke in. 'Sir Peter. Sir Peter. I just glimpsed the dog again, and a man beyond, going down through Larch Wood. They seem to be making off towards Foleyhill Quarry. They'll be our vandals, likely. If we moved quickly, we could maybe head them off. Over.'

'I'm not turning my day out into a vandal-hunt,' Sir Peter's voice said. 'And there's no need. Keith, where are you? Over.'

Keith pressed to transmit. 'I'm on the way down the valley, about half a mile before the quarry. They'll have to pass me or face some bloody rough walking.'

'Try and see them go by. I want descriptions, car numbers, anything. Molly says you still have her camera, so get a photograph if you can. But understand this, you're not to get physically involved. No having-a-go. And no threats with your gun. You read me? Over.'

'I got you,' Keith said. 'Not to worry. I'm well hidden where I am, and the way I feel it'd take more than a brace of vandals to get me to shift. I'll spot them for you. Over.'

'We'll leave it to you, then. Right, everybody, get ready for the next drive. Take over, Hamish.'

Keith switched off the radio in case sudden voices betrayed him and stowed it away in his pocket. He dragged himself round and on to his knees and then moved slightly to one side so that he could peer through the gap where a stone had fallen out of the top of the wall. He was partly screened by a rowan tree bright with berries and, as long as he made no sudden moves, his head would be imperceptible against the dark gorse on the slope behind him. He propped the camera on the wall, put his empty gun beside him and waited. After a minute he laid his forehead against the warm stones.

He must have dozed off. He woke with a jerk to the sound of footsteps, muted voices and irrepressible giggles. He raised his head cautiously.

Three people and a dog were approaching down the valley. There was no need for the camera. Keith already had photographs of all three – the girl, the young man who had met him at Foleyhill and the round-faced lad whom they had guessed to be the driver of the Capri in France. All three were dressed in clothes which seemed to have been chosen for their inconspicuous colours rather than with a view to suitability or comfort. The dog, a black and white collie, stayed close to the heel of the second man.

As they came abreast of Keith, the girl made some comment. Her voice was shaking with mirth and Keith could only make out the concluding words, '. . . something to grouse about.' All three spluttered with fresh laughter.

Still laughing, the girl stopped in her stride. 'You two walk on,' she said. 'I'll catch you up later.' She turned and seemed to be looking straight into Keith's face. He lowered his head slowly.

Voices and footsteps receded down the valley. Keith could not make out whether the girl was with them. All seemed silent beyond the wall. He gave Tanya a signal which would keep her anchored to the spot until summoned and got gently to his feet. There seemed to be no sign of the girl. He walked softly the few yards to the gateway and stepped through. He still felt weak but his exhaustion had retreated in the face of anger. These people had led him into a trap and, as if putting his life at risk had not been enough, were even now chortling over an attempt to wreck twenty men's sport for reasons which Keith could only consider to be malicious.

When he came through the gateway, Keith got the shock of his life. The girl was squatting almost at his feet. She had lowered a pair of pink pants and was quietly relieving herself into the grass. She was still laughing to herself. At Keith's sudden appearance, she looked up.

Keith said afterwards that if he had taken time to think he would have apologized and fled. But he acted without thinking, out of the depth of his anger. He aimed the camera and released the shutter.

Her laughter vanished, to be replaced by the sulky look which he remembered. She tried to pull down her short, brown skirt to retrieve some of her modesty.

Keith stepped forward. He reached out one foot and planted his boot on the pink pants, treading them into the damp grass and trapping her ankles. She glared up at him speechlessly. Her

100

tweed hat fell off and he saw that her hair, pinned up to go under the hat, had reverted to its original honey colour.

She came out of her first shock and pursed her lips to whistle.

'You call that dog,' Keith said, 'and I'll shoot it for sheep-worrying.'

She had been crouched, leaning back and supporting herself behind with one hand on the ground. She tried to lever herself forward, to get her balance for standing up. Keith advanced the barrels of his gun so that the tip of her nose entered one of the muzzles. He pushed gently. She subsided into her uncomfortable crouch but with both hands behind her. The sulky expression was submerged under indignant fury. 'You bastard!' she said. 'You proper *bastard*! Do you usually hold a gun on women?'

'I don't usually have to. Just at the moment you're probably stronger and faster than I am and I blame you for it. And I haven't used the gun yet. When I do, you won't feel a thing. You're sitting carelessly again,' he added.

She took one hand out from behind her and dragged at her skirt. The tension in the muscles of her other arm made her breasts quiver. 'I can make trouble,' she growled. 'I'll have you up for indecent assault.'

With his free hand Keith patted the camera which hung on his chest and he managed a sickly grin. 'I've got a good shot of you in here,' he said. He wondered whether Molly had loaded the camera. 'Squatting for a pee and smiling into the camera. How far do you think you could get in the face of that?'

'This is a hell of a way for a gentleman to treat a lady.' She tossed her head back to free her nose.

Keith waited until she was still again and then replaced the muzzle. 'I never pretended to be a gentleman,' he said. The anger mounting in him made it difficult to speak steadily. Her posture and the tantalizing glimpses which were being offered him would usually have roused his manhood to frenzy, but he felt nothing. If she and her friends had put paid to his sex-life, somebody was going to get hurt. He rotated the gun-barrels from left to right and back again, pressing harder. 'And you're a hell of a long way from being a lady,' he went on. 'If you hadn't tempted me up to Foleyhill with just the kind of lure you knew I couldn't resist, I wouldn't have a hole in my shoulder and I'd be able to handle you without a gun. And, by God, I'd give you the spanking you deserve. I just hope you're proud of yourself.'

She flushed and turned her head away. Keith rested the muzzles against her cheekbone. 'You were never meant to get hurt,' she said. 'That wasn't us. Somebody else must hate you as much as I do.'

'I worked that out for myself,' Keith said. 'You wanted to get a photograph of me skinning a poached deer in your sanctuary and use it to blackmail me.'

'Not for money!'

'I worked that out too. And you weren't going to force me to spare the lives of a few game birds and eat battery chickens instead, although that's the kind of

102

warped logic I'd expect from you. I can guess what you were after. What I can't figure out is why you wanted it. Are you going to tell me?'

The strain of her squatting position, leaning back on one hand with the other clutching at her skirt, was increasing. It showed in the dew of sweat on her forehead. She turned her head to glare at Keith and he trapped her nose in the muzzle again. 'You're so bloody clever,' she gasped, 'you find out.'

'I will,' Keith said. 'I certainly will. But you could save me time and effort. Or which would you rather be prosecuted for? Conspiracy to attempted murder? Attempted blackmail? Or inciting a dog to worry sheep? You name it. Perm any two from three.'

'You can't do that,' she ground out. 'You don't know who I am.'

Keith grinned to himself. 'No, I don't, do I?' With his left hand he drew out an envelope, one of several, from his inner pocket and held it up. 'I've been writing out the story as I discover it. There are copies at my bank and with my solicitor and I'm handing out copies to anyone who might still be under any delusion that knocking me off would suppress the story. Pass it on wherever you think fit.' He stepped back. 'You can go now.'

The girl pushed herself stiffly to her feet. Her moist and muddled panties clung to her ankles. She stepped out of them with a dignity that would have been a credit to a duchess, except that she had to shake one foot to dislodge the damp lace. She snatched the envelope from Keith's hand and walked away, surreptitiously, so she thought, easing her cramped muscles. Keith thought that she had the second finest bum in southern Scotland. She stopped and turned suddenly. 'You bastard!' she said again, but with deeper venom. 'I'm glad you got hurt. You've caused enough suffering!'

Keith regarded her with amusement. The tip of her nose was ringed with dark gun oil. 'Bastards don't die in their beds, you know,' he said mildly. 'Tell me, was that your brother with you?'

'You're so bloody clever –'

'I know. "Find out". The other one, was that Creepy Jesus?'

She almost smiled. 'If you ever meet Creepy, you'll know it.' She paused. 'How did you get that name?'

'You're so bloody clever,' Keith said, 'you find out. Keep your nose clean.' He grinned inwardly. His Parthian shot would only strike home when she reached a mirror.

As soon as she was out of sight he gingerly collected the abandoned pants and dropped them into his game bag.

Keith sat with his gun, loaded, across his knees until assured by the radio that Ronnie was on his way. Then he went gently on down, to find the quarry deserted. His exhaustion was now total. He was home, fed and in bed by mid-afternoon, and by the time that Molly returned, flushed with fresh air and good company, he was deep in sleep.

He awoke at dawn from a pleasing dream. He was never able to recapture the dream, although he thought that the fair girl had figured in it. He was suddenly aware that there was, at last, a great need in him. He turned to the warm body beside him.

Molly was adept at reading Keith's moods and responding to them. She pretended to struggle but was overborne.

Keith's outing, misguided as it was and flat against common sense and medical advice, should have set him back. But in fact it marked the beginning of his real recovery. He announced the imminent improvement – *after* being served his breakfast in bed – to Molly and Deborah.

'You'd better take it easy today,' Molly said briskly. 'But I can't wait on you. Janet and Wallace want to be relieved at the shop this afternoon.'

'Sit down,' Keith said. 'I've something to tell you which won't take a moment.' While Molly sat on the foot of the bed and Deborah crawled up the quilt and tried to pull his hair, he filled in the details of the day before, omitting very little. 'I suppose you think I was a bit hard on her,' he finished anxiously.

Molly would have been less pleased if Keith had treated Miss Duguidson with gentleness. 'If I'd been there I'd have taken the skin off her backside,' she said without hesitation. 'You wouldn't have been half-killed but for her. What you did was all right.'

Keith was reassured and encouraged. 'I'll be sending her an invitation to come for a chat as soon as the guns are here. It might just ram the message home if I sent her pants back to her at the same time.'

'It might,' Molly said. 'I wouldn't bet on it.'

'It's the least any gentleman could do. They're in my game bag. Could you give them a launder?'

Molly lifted Deborah off him. 'You've got a bloody nerve!' she said. But she was too relieved at the return of Keith's vitality to speak with any real heat.

Keith made no direct answer. He knew what kind of nerve he had. 'It's a pity we don't have a pair of Sir Henry's long-johns,' he said.

Keith cleared his tray of every crumb and bounced downstairs an hour later feeling on top of the world. 'I'll keep the shop this afternoon,' he announced.

'You're not fit,' Molly said reluctantly.

'Fit for anything.'

'That's what you said yesterday.'

'Yesterday I hoped it, but today I *feel* it.'

Molly sighed. 'We'll see if you can still keep your eyes open at lunchtime,' she said.

The weather outside was not tempting. Keith shut himself in the study. He sat down first at the word processor, intending to finalize the catalogue of antique guns. But he stared at the blank screen for a full minute. Instead of the catalogue, he called up his resumé and added conclusions drawn from the events of the previous day. He spent a few more seconds looking at the words which glinted from the screen.

He moved to the desk, opened the Yellow Pages and began to dial his way around the sporting goods shops. He was not optimistic. The crossbow could have been purchased by anybody, perhaps in the sports section of some superstore where memories would soon be trodden under the feet of a thousand customers. But it was worth a try.

So he started with the small shops. He varied his approach according to whatever he knew or could sense about the shop or its staff, but the burden of it remained the same. A crossbow had been left with him for repair. The defect was one of materials and he was trying to trace the original seller in order to invoke the guarantee.

To his astonishment, his eleventh call produced some positive responses. Yes, they stocked Barnett crossbows. Yes, they had sold at least one Commando recently. But no, it had been a cash sale and the proprietor had no recollection of the name or appearance of the purchaser.

'Does the nickname "Creepy Jesus" suggest anything?' Keith asked.

There was a pause. Keith had a vague recollection of the proprietor of the shop, and could imagine him blinking through thick lenses. 'Yes, by God!' said his voice suddenly. 'That describes him to a T. Tall, thin chap with a beard and fanatical eyes. Thin as a rake. And creepy. I'm not even sure he cast a shadow. He was only in here the once.'

'He bought the crossbow?'

'Yes. Definitely. He seemed to know what he was at. Made out that he was a bit of a marksman. Why didn't he bring it back to me?'

'Couldn't remember where he bought it,' Keith said. 'I'll send him back to you if he doesn't want to pay me for the repair.'

Keith broke off the call and returned to the word processor. He added the fresh information and ran off half a dozen new copies.

'I'd be glad of the afternoon to get on with things,' Molly said as she served his lunch. 'But are you safe, driving yourself?'

'I can manage,' Keith said. 'I'm more fashed about leaving you alone. I've tried to take the heat off, by letting it be known that killing me wouldn't hush anything up. But for God's sake take care and call the fuzz at the first sign of anything unfriendly. The last thing I could be doing with's a kidnapping.' He paused and frowned. 'I lent you a little Derringer once before,' he said. 'But I can't put my hand on it.'

Molly laid a finger between her breasts. 'I've already got it here,' she said.

'Well, that's something else to be careful about. I wouldn't love you so much with one tit shot off.'

'You're going to have to be more careful with that tongue of yours, my boy,' Molly said serenely. 'Deborah's beginning to take it all in.'

The shop was quiet. Keith kept himself occupied with a thin trickle of customers which dried up in the early afternoon. He was interrupted once by a phone-call to say that the coaster carrying his crated guns had docked at long last in Leith. He spent a few minutes in the basement, trying to puzzle out how on earth Wallace had achieved his extraordinary result on the barrels of Mr Threadgold's gun. Then, with little in prospect but the occasional request for catapult rubber, airgun pellets and fish hooks, he had nothing to do but to glower at some of Wallace's innovations. These might be good business, but they detracted from the shop as Keith preferred to remember it – a dignified establishment where gentlemen could meet to chat about guns and trout rods. He tried hard to ignore the bright row of skateboards on the topmost shelf.

It was a relief when the shop bell rang. Keith turned, smiling, to greet the new customer.

A man in drag walked into the shop. Keith blinked and looked again. By the articulation of hip and shoulder joints he realized that this was indeed a woman, but of such a stocky and masculine appearance as to make nylon hose, skirt and lacy blouse appear an indecent travesty.

'Mr Calder? I'm glad I've found you alone. I'm Lady Batemore.' Her voice, in startling contrast to her appearance, was feminine, even sexy and verging on erotic.

Keith came out from behind the counter and offered her the only chair. Then, rather than stand before her like a guilty schoolboy, he returned and busied himself tidying some catalogues. 'What can I do for you?' he asked.

'That is the question.' She glanced up at him. Her eyes, too, were feminine, but Keith thought that he could see dislike in their depths. Her voice, he noticed, had a trace of some Mediterranean accent. 'When you met my husband,' she went on, 'he made you an offer. Have you decided to accept it?'

Keith shook his head. 'No. Before I commit myself, I intend to find out a lot more than I know now. Which reminds me.' He pulled out a copy of his resumé. 'After I saw your husband, I was attacked and nearly killed. So I've been noting down what I know and handing it out, just to make it known that attacks on me won't hide anything.'

She dropped it unopened into her bag. 'I have already seen a copy.'

'I added to it this morning. My solicitor and bank manager have fresh copies.'

'I shall read it later. I assume that its content does not differ greatly from the earlier version. That was a statement of the facts as you knew them, but you went on to draw certain inferences. I would like to assure you, Mr Calder, that at least as far as my family is concerned those inferences are wrong.'

'But not actionable,' Keith said.

'No,' she agreed reluctantly. 'But there are further implications which you did not set down and which could be very harmful to us if anything were to happen to you.'

'Then it'd be best, for all our sakes, that nothing happens to me. Is this what you came to talk about?'

'No. I came in the hope that I might be able to improve on my husband's offer to you, and perhaps to persuade you to accept it. Would you be willing to show me your list of the guns from France?'

'I don't see why not; I'll be re-issuing my catalogue soon anyway.' Keith was still carrying his pencilled draft, awaiting a chance to discuss it with Wallace. He passed it across.

Lady Batemore ran her eye down it eagerly. 'Several of these guns are still unpriced,' she said.

'Those ones won't be going into my catalogue until I've investigated further or done some repair work.'

'I understand. This miquelet musket, decorated with copper nails, is that the one which you bought from a family named Detournville, near Lizerche?' Keith felt his hands jump. She must have seen the movement, because she smiled. 'I have many business interests in France,' she said. 'It was not difficult to have your movements traced. Tell me, what is a miquelet?'

Keith felt himself back on firmer ground. 'An early form of flintlock, developed in Spain. It was soon superseded, but the Spanish remained faithful to it for a couple of hundred years. In fact, the style was popular all round the Mediterranean, especially in Arab countries. You can tell it by the short, straight-stemmed cock with a ring-headed screw at the top, and by the external main springs. It was probably the first lock to combine the steel with the flashpancover –'

'That's enough,' she barked. (Keith stopped dead, blinking. How could anybody not want to hear the fascinating history of the miquelet lock, and its important place in the evolution of the gun?) 'These duelling pistols, are these the ones by C. J. Ross of Edinburgh? The ones found in the coach in the barn?'

'They are.'

'You avoided mention of them when you spoke to my husband.'

'I didn't avoid mentioning them,' Keith said. 'I just didn't single them out for mention.'

Their discussion was broken by the arrival of a customer to collect a set of chokes for his repeater. Lady Batemore spent the interval studying Keith's list. When the door closed again she said, 'You charge high prices, Mr Calder.'

'They're valuable guns, Lady Batemore.'

'My husband made you an offer for his choice of any two guns. He may have erred on the miserly side. Suppose I were to repeat his offer for my choice of any one gun, or double it for my choice of any three?'

Keith began, yet again, to revise his theories. 'And for any two guns?' he asked tentatively.

They settled down to haggle. Her ladyship proved to be as dedicated as her husband.

'Do we have a deal?' she asked at last.

Keith decided to keep his options open. 'Today,' he said, 'is Thursday. I'll make a decision on Saturday morning. The day after tomorrow. Please invite Sir Henry to be at my house by ten-thirty a.m. You'll meet old friends. The Duguid-sons.'

Lady Batemore threw up her head and snorted. 'Certainly not,' she said. 'Those two are little better than criminals. You would be ill advised to do any business with them.'

'Come at twelve, then. I'll see them separately.'

'But you won't dispose of anything to them before you've seen us?'

'I doubt if the question will arise.'

'We'll be there. I take it that the guns are now in this country?'

'Oh yes. They're in this country.'

She stood up. 'Good afternoon,' she said.

As soon as he could decently close the shop, Keith went in search of his brother-in-law.

As it turned out, Molly's brother expected to be away on Sir Peter's business the next day and his Land Rover with him. Keith made a firm arrangement for Saturday morning and drove home.

'Fancy a day's shopping in Edinburgh?' he asked Molly.

'Silly question,' she answered. Keith knew that nothing short of his funeral or her own would come between Molly and the chance of a day among the bright lights of Princes Street.

CHAPTER EIGHT

The prospect of physical danger to himself had never worried Keith; nor was he overly concerned about most of his personal possessions. But because of the historical and cash value of the guns under the Briesland House roof, and also the possibility that these might attract intruders who would pose a threat to Molly and such children as she might bear, he had installed the latest and best fire and burglary alarms. But, because he was always interested in knowing who might be casting covetous glances in his direction and why, he had, with the aid of a friend skilled in modern electronics, added a refinement of his own. This permitted the optional inclusion of a delay between those virtually silent infra-red intruder-alarms on the ground floor going off and the yodelling electronic siren on the roof starting up.

So it was by a discreet buzz that Keith (and not the entire neighbourhood) was awakened in the middle of the night. At first he thought that he was only hearing the alarm-clock and he prepared to ignore it, but Molly jerked him awake with a cruel elbow.

'Keith! We're being burgled!'

Reluctantly, Keith levered his mind up out of its nest of slumber and fumbled for his slippers. He opened the door very gently and tiptoed to the head of the stairs. Bright moonlight lay across the hall. The intruder was still on the ground floor or the alarm would have gone off in earnest; but he had a margin of two minutes from the first intimation until the siren sounded, after which the cottager at the market garden would phone the police and claim a promised bottle of whisky.

Keith waited, with bowel-watering impatience, while the hall clock ticked away his time. He did not want Chief Inspector Munro poking his long, Hebridean nose in. Nor was he anxious to part with a bottle of whisky to the undeserving and rather smelly old man in the market garden cottage. But he had not the least intention of going downstairs until he knew precisely where the other man was.

A sound came from below him; stealthy fumbling followed by a double click and then the whisper of a door opening. The intruder would pass immediately beneath him. Keith had one of his duelling pistols in his hand. He knew that he could easily lean over the banisters and bat the intruder over the head with it, but because of the twin risks of an accidental discharge and of damage to a valuable gun he preferred not to. He laid the pistol softly down on a nearby table and instead picked up a solid ornament, ostensibly of bronze, a wedding present from one of Molly's relatives. Molly set some store by it, but Keith did not. It portrayed a knight in armour rescuing a naked damsel from some unspecified peril. Something about the knight's attitude suggested that his intent was less than honourable, although a full suit of armour was hardly ideal garb for such pastimes. Keith considered it vulgar without being funny, but well suited for dropping on the heads of burglars passing beneath.

Keith knew that, contrary to popular belief, there is a dangerously small margin between the force of blow which will stun a man and that which will kill him. The man might be thin-skulled. As a dark figure appeared below, Keith made a guess and lowered his hands slightly. Then he saw the silhouette of a sawn-off shotgun and raised his hands almost to full stretch before letting go.

The flat base of the bronze descended accurately on the man's skull. The noise would have been sickening, but Keith was unable to hear it. The alarm siren chose that instant to burst into its wobbling wail.

Keith went down the stairs in a series of leaps, deciding as he went what he was going to do. He knew precisely his proper course of action, but had not the least intention of sticking to it.

He jerked open the hall cupboard and punched the code to silence the alarm. He was almost certainly too late. His neighbour, who had been known to doze off at the wheel of a tractor, was almost insomniac when there was whisky in prospect. Keith's ears sang in the sudden silence.

The intruder was out but seemed to be breathing naturally. Keith seized him by the ankles, dragged him through a door and let him bump heavily down the stairs into the former kitchen now a utility room.

116

Keith grabbed Molly's spare clothes line and slashed it into random lengths with a carving knife. The man was already beginning to stir. Keith was not disposed to be clement. With vicious jerks he knotted the man's wrists behind him, and then tied his ankles together and connected them to his wrists with a generous length of line. Finally, he used a folded duster as a gag and bound it in place with several turns of line. By this time the man's eyes – fanatic's eyes, Keith thought, sunk deep in the skull under the weight of venom – were open and glaring unsteadily.

'Don't go away,' Keith said. 'The police are just coming. If you make enough noise you might be able to get their attention. I can think of several reasons why you'd better not. You can probably think of many more.'

Keith hurried upstairs to the hall. Molly was leaning over the banisters. 'Keith, what's happening?'

Light washed in through the window as a car turned on the gravel forecourt. 'All's well,' Keith said. 'Just hang on. Leave the talking to me.' Hastily, he scooped up the bronze and set it on the hall table. Its descent had subtly altered the posture of the figures. The maiden was now slightly bow-legged and her head seemed to be cocked in anticipation. The knight's buttocks now protruded as if he were trying to find more room in his armour. Keith decided that the ornament was improved.

He unchained the front door and opened it. Two constables were emerging from a panda car. 'We had a burglar, but he's away empty-handed,' Keith said.

One constable returned to the car and the radio. The other walked past Keith into the house, looked in surprise at the bronze ornament, sat down beside the hall table and opened his notebook. Molly had withdrawn from sight but not, Keith guessed, from earshot.

'You were quick,' Keith said.

'We were out this way, sir. What happened?'

Keith had not had time to think. He edited his story as he went along. 'I was woken by the alarm,' he said. 'I rushed to the head of the stairs. There was a man in the hall, unlocking the front door. The alarm going off seemed to have scared him out of his wits. I'm not surprised, it makes one hell of a din. Anyway, he got the door open and rushed out.'

'You're sure he took nothing?'

'He'd no time, and he wasn't carrying anything large.'

'You'll let us know if you find that anything's missing. . . . Did you get a good look at him?'

Keith thought. He had not taken in the man's appearance, but it came back to him piecemeal. 'Tall, over six feet,' he said. 'Thin. I mean thinly built and fleshless with it. Dark hair and . . .' yes, he remembered it getting in the way of the gag '. . . a straggly beard.' As he gave the description, he recognized it. And he decided to stretch his luck. 'He looked like some Biblical character, except that he was wearing a dark sweater and jeans.'

The constable took it all down. 'How did he get in?' he asked.

Keith thought back to the noise which he had heard while he waited on the landing. 'I don't know until I look,' he said. 'But there's a sort of back hall. The dogs sleep there and there's a dog door cut through the bigger outside door. We lock the inner door but he may have picked it.'

The constable looked disbelieving. 'Surely he wouldn't have come past two dogs without waking you?'

'Those two greedy lumps would ignore the Second Coming if somebody threw them a lump of meat.'

'We'd better take a look.'

Keith tried the door to the back hall and switched on the light. The two dogs, instead of bouncing forward in welcome, lay inert on the floor. Keith squatted and got up again. 'Molly,' he called.

'Yes,' from overhead.

'Call the vet. Ask him to get here as soon as he can. The dogs have been doped. Barbiturates, probably.'

'Are they going to be all right?'

'That's for the vet to tell us.'

'All right.'

'Just as well that you have the alarms,' the constable said. He finished his examination of the back hall. 'Somebody from C.I.D. will come out first thing and take a look around.'

'Ask him to make it before ten. We're going into Edinburgh.'

'The vet's on his way,' Molly broke in. She was leaning on the banister above them.

The constable paused on his way through the hall and bent down to reach under the hall table. 'Hullo!' he said. 'Nearly missed this against the pattern of the carpet. I'd have got stick if I had. A sawn-off shotgun, by God! We don't see many of those in this neck of the woods. The numbers may help.'

'Let Keith see it,' Molly said. 'He may recognize it. He never forgets a gun.' Keith thought that there was something in her voice. She was up to something.

'Yes?' The constable sounded doubtful, but he turned round with the gun in his hands.

Keith took it from him and unloaded two BB cartridges from it. 'It belongs,' he said, 'to a Mr Threadgold of Bonnyrigg. You might ask him whether he recognizes my description of the man.'

'We've had no report of a gun being stolen in Bonnyrigg,' said the constable.

'If it was pinched out of his car he may not have missed it yet,' Keith said.

As soon as the door closed behind the policeman, Molly came skittering down the stairs. She looked delicious in a frilly nightdress and negligee, both almost transparent, and Keith was glad that she had stayed in the background. 'You're up to something,' she said. 'I can tell. What is it?'

'Come and see.'

Keith led the way down the stairs. Molly gasped when she saw the man on the floor, struggling against her clothes line.

'Just stand by,' Keith said. 'Trust me for one minute. Then I'll explain.' He went down on his knees. With his last length of cord he tied a bowline

120

round the man's neck and checked it carefully to be sure that it would never slip. 'You poor chap!' he said. 'Let me help you up.'

With Keith's help the man got on to his feet, but before he could stand fully erect the link between his wrists and ankles came taut. Quickly, Keith attached the rope from the man's neck to an overhead pulley which more usually supported a clothes drier.

'I haven't much time,' Keith said, 'so I'll say it just once. I'm going to take the gag out for about ten seconds. In that time, if you want a good puke, you've got your chance. But you also tell me what drug you gave my dogs. Otherwise, if one of them dies, you can have a share in the grave.'

'You can't do that,' Molly protested. 'Keith, you *can't*—'

Upstairs, the front door bell began to ring.

'Before you get too uptight,' Keith said, 'you may as well know that this is the nutter who stuck me with the crossbow bolt. If I hadn't been turning at that moment, he'd've killed me.' Keith untied the cord and removed the duster. 'Now then, Creepy Jesus, you've got one chance and only one to tell me what you gave my dogs.'

Creepy Jesus's face above the beard was greenish grey and his wild eyes seemed unfocused, but the message had got through to him. He groaned out two faint syllables. Keith made out the name of a well-known sleeping tablet.

Keith hesitated and then threw down the gag. He handed Molly her rolling pin from a drawer. 'Stand guard,' he said. 'If he tries to shout, zonk him with this. Try not to kill him too much. Then cut him down before he hangs himself.' He saw that Molly was swinging rapidly from sympathy with the oppressed to indignation that anybody should dare to take up arms against her beloved Keith. 'But as long as he stands there quietly, leave him be.'

Molly nodded uncertainly.

'Promise me? In words?' (Keith never considered a non-verbal promise binding.)

'I promise,' she said.

Keith darted back up the stairs and admitted the vet, whom he found, in overcoat and pyjamas, about to doze off on the doorstep. 'Did Molly tell you we've had an intruder? He doped the dogs. I found the empty bottle,' Keith improvised. He repeated the name furnished by Creepy Jesus.

Keith hovered anxiously while the vet examined the sleeping dogs and gave each an injection. 'Just leave them as they are,' the vet said at last. 'They should make it through the night. It's a bit by-guess-and-by-God, because we don't know how much they were given. But if they're not both up and around by midday, call me again.' He yawned. 'I should get such a sleep!' he added.

Keith took him to the door and pointed him in the direction of his car.

In his younger days Keith had lived on the fringe of a world in which it was the custom first to demand information with threats and then to offer violence. Keith knew that physical attack must often fail, simply because it is finite and must end some time. The determined victim can stick it out. Keith's interlude with the girl in the valley had suggested to him another way to extract information. Much more effective, he thought, would be the pain from within one's own muscles, pain which would continue to escalate until ended by capitulation.

The desired result seemed already near when Keith returned downstairs. Under the eye of an unsympathetic Molly, Creepy Jesus was suffering. As an alternative to taking his weight on his throat he was forced to take the strain on his bent legs. The effort demanded of his legs and back was already evident in his sweating face and his laboured breathing. Soon, Keith knew, over-strained muscles would begin to share the strain with other muscles less well adapted to the particular task, violently increasing the load on the skeletal joints.

Keith pulled out a chair and sat down facing his captive. Molly perched on the corner of the table. While Keith spent a few seconds considering the order of his approach, there was a silence broken only by Creepy Jesus's gasping breaths. Yet Keith noticed that those wild eyes kept flicking in Molly's direction. Had she said or done something while he was out of the room?

'I think you should go back to bed,' Keith told Molly.

'I'm staying.'

'All right. But cover yourself. I want his full attention.'

Molly got up, put on an old macintosh from behind the back door and resumed her seat on the table.

'Now,' Keith said. Creepy Jesus's eyes settled back on him, like insects. 'Did you ever play tiddlywinks?' Keith asked.

'Hunh?'

'Because you're going to have discs popping out all over the place just like that if you don't get loose soon. And the only way you get loose is by spilling all you know.'

'You're not going to let him *go*?' Molly said incredulously.

'I might, if he's a good boy.'

'Keith, you've got to give him up to the police. He tried to *kill* you.'

Keith moved his shoulder experimentally. It was still slightly tender. 'I can't prove that he tried to kill me,' he said. 'Only that he bought a crossbow. He might get off on that. And it's a bit late to let on that I caught the burglar. And, finally, if I throw him to the cops the whole story's going to come out and I'm not ready for that yet. At least, I don't think I am.' Keith returned his attention to Creepy Jesus. 'What've you got to say for yourself, Sunshine?'

The man glared at him. Keith would not have believed that two eyes, mere globes of soft tissue, could hold so much hate together with so little real sanity. His speech, it turned out, was out-dated American slang, intended to be hippy-talk and delivered in a strong Glasgow twang horribly discordant with his Christ-like appearance. He spoke in a series of short breaths as he fought the increasing strain on his body. 'I don't have to . . . tell you a word, man.'

'You don't,' Keith agreed. 'You can hang there instead. Be my guest.'

A few seconds of silence and cramp persuaded Creepy Jesus to speak again. 'No need to . . . blow cool. Don't know what . . . word you want.'

'What did you come here for?'

'Who you tryin' . . . to kid? . . . I was hoping to score . . . with those shooters. . . . The ones by C. J. Ross . . . from France.'

'You're sure you didn't fancy your chances at knocking me off? You tried once before.'

'Christ no! Hey, man . . . what the hell! . . . You wrote down that I'd . . . had first crack at you. An' I didn't,' he added suddenly but too late. 'I'd've been easy meat for the fuzz. Just wanted . . . enough bread . . . to take me away to hell and gone. . . . Let me down, man . . . this is killing me.'

'Probably. Tough titty. You bought the crossbow.'

Creepy Jesus hesitated and then capitulated. 'Okay, so I bought the crossbow for . . . for somebody else.'

'Just about everybody else I can think of is accounted for. Who would you like to nominate?'

'Not saying.'

'You may be sorry. Who were you going to sell the pistols to?'

'Highest bidder. . . . Cut me down, man.'

Keith thought it over and then shook his head. 'No, you had a client.'

'The girl, man,' Creepy Jesus said desperately. 'The Duguidson chick.'

'How much did she offer you to kill me?'

Creepy Jesus tried to clamp his mouth shut, but the snarl on his face left his sharp teeth showing.

'I don't buy it,' Keith said. 'I think the only word of truth you've told me is that your back hurts. Which moves me not one damn bit, because somebody put a crossbow bolt through me, meaning to kill me, and in my book it all adds up to you. Well, I don't have to hand you over to the cops. I gave them a hair-by-hair and pimple-by-pimple description of you and pointed them in the direction of Bonnyrigg. I don't suppose they'll knock up Mr Threadgold during the night, but come breakfast time they'll have your number. If I let you go – and I don't advise you to start counting on it – but *if* I were to let you go now and you started running straight away, you might have time to screw some money out of your client and be gone before the hunt warms up. But if you don't start telling me something I can believe you can bloody well wait here until morning and think about your sins.' Keith got to his feet.

'I'll be dead . . . by then!'

'Probably. Who shot me with the crossbow? I want to hear it from your own lips. And,' Keith said, 'if you think that the idea of you dying bothers me you're living in a dream world.'

Creepy Jesus rolled his eyes but failed to find any help. 'All right, you mother!' he said. 'It was me shot you.'

'Now tell me something new.'

'All I know is . . . those shooters, man . . . the pistols . . . they've got a history . . . Val and Hugh,

126

they found out something . . . last year . . . at the family mansion in France.'

'Oh, I knew that,' Keith said. 'I guessed something like that from the first, and I knew I was right as soon as Sir Henry tried to buy them. But now I'm guessing that that's yesterday's news. What else can you tell me?'

Creepy Jesus shook his head so that sweat flew.

'Too bad,' Keith said. 'If you don't make it through the night I'll dig a grave between the lilacs and dance on it from time to time. That's what I think of men who try to kill me. A good night to you. If you think of anything else, try shouting. I'm two floors up, but you might just manage to wake me.'

In the morning the man was gone. Keith made the utility room his first port of call and found only a few cut strands of rope. Molly had followed Keith to bed after twenty minutes during which, armed with the carving knife in case she had to defend herself, she had cut Creepy Jesus free, as Keith had been almost sure she would.

It seems unlikely that Creepy Jesus ever knew how lucky he was. During the night the old spaniel's heart had given out under the strain. So there was a grave between the lilacs after all, but no dancing.

It was a late start that they made for Edinburgh, but Keith made up time on the road and dropped his wife and daughter, nervous but glad to be uninjured, at the West End with instructions to work their way along Princes Street and then to seek out the car on a meter in Queen Street or York Place.

Keith spent the morning arguing with the Customs and Excise at Leith over the import of his guns. He snatched a bite of lunch in the St James Centre and spent the afternoon in Register House.

Molly had found the car by the time Keith returned to it and had established herself in the driving seat. Deborah was already strapped into her own seat in the back. Keith settled himself down beside Molly. For once he was disinclined to assert his male prerogative to drive. 'I got what I wanted,' he said with satisfaction.

'You got more than you wanted,' Molly said. 'There was a summons under your wiper.'

'That's not mine,' Keith said. 'Throw it away. I pinched it off somebody else's windscreen. Traffic wardens don't bother if they see that you've already got a summons. Let's get along home. I want to phone the university. And then I'd like to ask Mrs Threadgold what the legal question that Valerie Duguidson asked her husband was, as if I couldn't guess.'

CHAPTER NINE

By ten-thirty on the Saturday morning, Keith was beginning to feel that the week had already gone on long enough. One cause among many was that his study was in a state of congested disorder. Keith had been reared in a farmhouse among utilitarian furniture and whitewash, and however much he might decry Molly's veneration for Briesland House it gave him eternal satisfaction to have a room to himself which could almost have figured in a Stately Home.

Ronnie and a companion had delivered four large crates to the study and were being regaled by Molly in the kitchen while Keith began the process of opening the crates.

The Duguidsons arrived – ahead of time, Keith noted. Molly, determined as ever to miss no moment of drama, got rid of her brother and joined the party but caused a further delay by offering refreshments.

Keith glared at her. 'I did not invite these two young yobs here in order to feed them,' he pointed out.

Molly remembered that those two had lured

129

Keith almost to his death. She also remembered that she had been quite unable to extract from Keith a single word about what he was expecting to be said or done. 'What did you invite these two young yobs here for then?' she asked.

'Not to be insulted,' the girl said. She got to her feet.

Her brother caught her by the sleeve without getting up. He had arrived in a mood of nervous garrulity but had then dried up. Now he found his voice again. 'Let's get it over,' he said huskily. 'I've been scunnered of the whole thing ever since it happened, and then you getting your pants back through the post and knowing that he – you – knew who we are. . . . Go on, Mr Calder, for God's sake. The floor's yours.'

'Since what happened?' Molly asked.

'Since Mr Calder got injured, of course,' Valerie Duguidson said impatiently. She sat slowly down again. 'That's what he means.'

Her brother took over again. 'All right, I met you and took you up to Foleyhill. We had nothing against you, but our need seemed paramount at the time. Call me anything you want. But, honestly, nobody was meant to get hurt, we just wanted to be able to put some pressure on you to sell us something at the same price you paid for it.'

Keith thought that Hugh Duguidson was trying to stretch credulity rather far. 'Whose idea was it?' he asked.

'Creepy suggested it. And he bought the cross-bow and shot the deer. He denied shooting at you, but he's lost the crossbow and with Creepy you

130

never know whether he's telling the truth or not. If he did it, we don't know what got into him or who got at him. So you needn't blame us. Anyway, you got your own back on Val and you can take a poke at me if you want, so you don't have to be too vindictive about it.'

'I don't have to be,' Keith agreed. 'Whether I will be or not depends on whether I get a little collaboration from you. For starters, tell me what this is all about.'

The boy opened his mouth but the girl spoke quickly. 'There's a story attached to those pistols which –'

'Wrong!' Keith sang on a long note.

'It's true! It makes them more valuable. To me, both as a student and as a member of the family –'

'Almost true, but it's not what you're so het up about. You'll have to do better if I'm not to go to my old friend Chief Inspector Munro and say that I now know who lured me up to Foleyhill so that their resident nutter could put a bolt through me. Let's start again. We'll take it more or less in chronological order. You two are remote cousins of the Batemores?'

The two youngsters nodded in unison.

'About a year ago,' Keith went on, 'you spent a holiday in Lady B.'s château. The Batemores don't take much interest in you, so I suppose that was young Brian's doing. Don't bother denying it. Your pal Creepy let it out. And the Batemores will be here later, I can ask them.'

'What of it, then?' It was the girl again. That sulky look, Keith thought, spoiled her face.

131

'Just this. You're a postgraduate history student – I asked the university. You're working on a thesis subject to do with French history. Lady Batemore's lineage is an inseparable part of that history. Her family archives or muniments or whatever you call them would be just your cup of tea. Your cousin would be sure to give you access to them.'

'Why not?'

'No reason. Creepy Jesus tried to buy me off with the story of you finding a letter or something among the family papers. He said that it was about the duelling pistols.'

'All right,' she said despondently. 'You win.'

'You're still trying, aren't you? But you needn't be quite so determined to get sent to prison. We can arrange it with half the effort. Those duellers are not, repeat not, what it's all about, and you know it. You had the bloody nerve to scrounge free advice from Mr Threadgold, who you and your unwashed commune had been persecuting. You asked him for a legal opinion. He told you that what you'd been thinking just wasn't on.'

'He could be wrong,' she said.

'He could, but he wasn't. I've asked my own solicitor. And there's another thing. When Lady B. came to the shop the other day, our discussion was informative. She offered me a big inducement in return for first pick of any three guns and a not much reduced offer for any one gun. When I suggested any two guns, she went tepid on me. So I reasoned that she wanted the duellers, but she wanted something else a damned sight more.

Probably something which she might never have known about if you hadn't drawn it to her attention by pinching something else out of the family archives – a document which she intended to recover either through the courts or through her son, who has the run of your doss-house.'

From the odds-and-ends drawer in his desk Keith produced a small pistol of the Derringer type. He sighted it at a corner of the ceiling. 'As a collector's piece,' he said, 'this would hardly seem to be worth the stamp on a cheque. But suppose I told you that this was the pistol Abraham Lincoln was killed with.'

'Keith!' Molly said. 'It isn't? – '

'No, of course it's not. I'm just trying to get across the difference in values, from a collector's point of view, between a poor antique and an historic item. When I'm looking at guns I might buy, I always have in my mind that one of them may have figured in a famous killing or have belonged to somebody in the history books. I've only scored once and that was in a small way. I've another gun upstairs which I'm hanging on to, because I suspect that it once belonged to a famous explorer but I can't prove it yet. I'm saying all this to explain that the possibilities were already in my mind when I bought these guns, and, as soon as Lady Batemore gave me the clue, my mind jumped to one gun in particular – partly because the man who sold it to me mentioned the *"deux pauvres étudiants"* who'd been after it. You two amateurs pushed the price up to a level which I wouldn't have paid, except that the resemblance to a certain famous and well-documented gun was almost jumping up and down in front of me, screaming for attention.'

Keith dropped the Derringer back into his drawer and got to his feet. He laid aside the lid from one of his long packing cases, lifted out several wrapped and labelled guns to uncover another which he laid on his desk while he repacked the case. There was silence in the room, expectant and anxious, while he slit the tapes and carefully unwrapped the padded paper until the gun was laid bare.

It would have looked like a poor relation even among Sir Henry's gallery of unimportant guns, a long musket with the wooden stock weatherbeaten, cracked and wormy, the metalwork eroded with rust. Yet even after its long eclipse it had a strong and purposeful look. The style, with its short, straight cock topped by the ring-headed screw, looked foreign even to unskilled eyes.

'You were after this,' Keith said. 'So also were Lady Batemore and Creepy Jesus. As it stands, and in this condition, it's worth comparatively little – old miquelets were common enough in Spanish and Mediterranean countries. Yet this is a very special gun.

'You two will know at least part of the story. But I don't think Molly knows it, so I'm going to run over the history of the gun which I think has now surfaced.'

Keith had placed a small stack of books on the corner of his desk, each holding a paper marker. He opened them in a line across the desk. 'We go right back to the Spanish conquest of central America,' he said. 'After Cortés and Pizarro and de Quesada, when they were exploring northward. Francisco de Coronado records that one of his captains, one Miguel Zegarra, had brought out to him a gun in the new Spanish style by the great Simon Marquarte. The same gun is mentioned in the *Compendio Historico de los arcabuceros de Madrid*, and Solér mentions that it bore Marquarte's trademark, a sickle, which,' Keith said, 'is about the only original marking you can still make out on this tatty object. It can be traced through several engagements up to and including the one in which Zegarra fell and the gun was taken by a famous Apache chief. After that it disappeared for more than a century.

'In 1710 a famous massacre took place at Broken Flats, near Lake Charles in Louisiana.' Keith switched books again. 'According to contemporary accounts some Frenchmen had been trading with a party of Tonkawa Indians under a chief named Chondo. After they parted, Chondo discovered that his most treasured possession had been stolen. This was a miquelet musket, which he had won in personal combat from an Apache chief whose grandfather had himself captured it from the Spaniards. Chondo is said to have decorated the stock, after the manner of the plains Indians, with a design in copper nails representing his own emblem, the otter.' Keith's hand stroked the ancient wood. The pattern of copper nails included an outline which resembled an otter as much as it did any other creature.

'The Indians set off in pursuit and came up with the Frenchmen at Broken Flats. Accounts of the fight differ –' Keith changed books again – 'but the general consensus is that it lasted for three days. The Indians outnumbered the French, but the French were better armed. At close of play, only one Indian and three of the French survived.

'That story is one of the classics of early America and any American collector would give both his ears for Chondo's gun. You think, and I think, that this is it. Now what have you got to say?'

Miss Duguidson raised her chin and glared at the ceiling.

'Tell him,' her brother said tiredly.

She switched her glare to him. 'You keep out of this, you . . . you *poltroon!*'

'I am sick to hell of all this,' the boy answered. 'We keep getting in deeper and deeper. It's been costing us money that we haven't got in the hope of something that we haven't a hope of getting. God alone knows what Creepy's been getting up to and I just don't want to know any more, but if we go on like this we're going to be in it with him. Mr Calder, you're right all along the line.

'Brian invited us over. His parents weren't there and we thought that he had their permission. Val was going through a chest full of old papers in the corner of their library, looking for material for her thesis, when she came across a letter from Louisiana. It was signed, "*Votre cousin, Jules Bonnier*".'

Keith looked down at one of his books. 'One of the survivors at Broken Flats was called Bonner or Bonnier,' he said.

'That figures. He mentioned some gifts and curios which he was sending home or to friends. And he said that he was sending a Spanish gun in the

136

miquelet style, but decorated with nails after the manner of the plains Indians, to his brother-in-law, Henri Detournville.'

'And I bought the gun from a man named Detournville,' Keith said. 'That ties it up very nicely.'

'They could use your mouth as a model for the Channel Tunnel,' Valerie told her brother sourly. 'Well, you know most of it, Mr Calder, so you may as well know the rest. I'd been reading up about the Louisiana French and I knew the story of Broken Flats. I guessed that the letter could transform a very ordinary antique into a collector's dream. Then the old bitch arrived and kicked up stink about us being there at all. So I hung on to the letter and one of the servants told her about it. She told Brian to get it back from me or else. He tried to coax it out of me, but I wasn't playing. Instead, I said I'd cut him in on what I could get if I could buy the gun. His parents pay his bills, but they keep him chronically short of ready cash; so my guess is that the bastard decided to go after the gun for himself and then either to hold me to ransom or try to pinch the letter off me.

'Anyway, the letter told us where to go. Monsieur Detournville – the present one – still had the gun, hanging on the wall in a disused room among some old swords and bits of armour and animal heads. We tried to buy it but, just as you said, we must have seemed too eager and he set the price too high for us. We spent the year trying to raise the wind, and we were nearly there when that piece appeared in *The Scotsman*.

'Brian was in a tizzy about those pistols – that's another story – and he shot over to France. And he phoned to say that you'd also bought our miquelet.'

'Whose?' Keith asked gently.

The girl half-smiled. Her attitude had become almost friendly. 'Well, we thought of it as ours. If Brian thought we were going to give up, he was wrong. We set off as soon as we could. Nobody'd say where you were, so we watched Riberac –'

'Yes, we figured out the rest,' Keith said. 'So your motives were purely financial. And when you didn't manage to steal the gun out of our car you decided to lure me up to Foleyhill for purposes of framing and blackmail.'

'But,' she said earnestly, 'we didn't intend any violence and we don't know anything about it. Creepy denied everything, but you can't believe a word he says. He had the crossbow, but we can't think why he should use it like that. Can you?'

'Let's not concern ourselves with what I can or can't think of.'

'Well, I'd have a job believing that it was because you'd deflowered his sister,' Valerie said, 'because if he has one she wouldn't be a virgin and he wouldn't mind anyway.'

'And if she was and he did,' Keith said, 'I didn't.'

'If he did and she was and you did,' Molly said coldly, 'you probably wouldn't remember.'

Keith was nearly distracted into arguing that, whatever he might have been in the past, he was now a happily – and faithfully – married man. But he held to the more important point. 'Where is the letter now?' he asked.

Valerie hesitated but her brother chimed in. 'She's got it with her. You said to bring whatever-it-was, and I insisted.'

She gave him a look which, Keith thought, would have fired a matchlock. 'So I've got it with me,' she said. 'So what?'

'You're probably thinking that you can make me pay for it,' Keith said. 'But, now that you've given me the connection, I've only got to go back through the parish records and prove that Bonnier had a brother-in-law named Detournville and I've got a provenance which would satisfy most collectors. No way are you getting the gun off me at a price which would make room for a profit. So leave the letter with me and I may not say anything to the police about stolen property, nor about you having set me up at Foleyhill. The letter's worthless to you without the gun.'

She took out a cigarette-lighter. 'And suppose I set fire to it?'

'Then I call the police. Destroying stolen property is a serious charge on its own. Make your mind up quickly. The Batemores will be arriving soon, and if Lady B. hears that you've got her letter with you she'll howl so loud for the cops that they'll hear her in Newton Lauder without benefit of a telephone.'

His sister sat as if made of stone but Hugh Duguidson got to his feet. 'I don't know about you, Val,' he said, 'but I'm for off. If there's anything I want less than to meet the old dragon again, I can't think of it.'

The girl got to her feet. She was shaking with anger. She took from her bag three small pages of stained paper, each covered with cramped writing and each now separately preserved between two sheets of plastic, and almost threw them at Keith. 'You bastard!' she said. 'You utter bastard! Stay away from Foleyhill. And I hope I never see your revolting face again,' she flung over her shoulder.

Keith watched her go, and he sighed. He hated to quarrel with anyone whose hips swung so bewitchingly. 'My photograph of you came out very well,' he said. 'I shall treasure it always.'

Hugh started to follow his sister but paused at the study door. 'Don't think too badly of her,' he said. 'You've had your revenge. When she opened your parcel, I thought she was going to wet her other pants.'

CHAPTER TEN

Sir Henry and his lady demonstrated their unconcern by being a calculated twenty minutes late, which gave Molly time to check that Deborah was still peacefully asleep and Keith time to carry out the next stage of his uncrating. He also opened a can of beer. Talking was thirsty work and there was more of it to come.

Lady Batemore, in feminine frills, was serene in her ugliness. She looked askance at Keith's half-empty beer-can. Sir Henry looked disdainfully around Keith's usually dignified study, which now looked less than its best. Neither of them glanced at Chondo's gun, which was laid along the mantelpiece, nor at the stained and warped mahogany case on the desk. They just sat, silent and imposing. Keith was seeing them together for the first time. He could well believe that they were cousins, pug-faced and highly-coloured.

Molly rejoined them. She took one quick look at the Batemores and then chose a chair outside the line of fire. Power and wealth, which only tended to raise Keith's hackles, overawed her.

Sir Henry waited until Keith opened his mouth to

speak and then got in first. 'I take it,' he said, 'that this means you've decided to accept my offer?'

'You can take it,' Keith replied, 'that I've decided not to. But we may still be able to do business once I've tied up some loose ends. Where is your son, by the way? I'd been hoping to see him here today.'

'He's abroad again,' Lady Batemore said.

Keith had a suspicion that it might be a long time before Brian Batemore set foot again on British soil. 'First of all,' he said, 'I think that I should return this to you. I don't deal in stolen goods.' And, with a queasy feeling that he was casting on the waters bread which might very well sink like a stone, he handed to Lady Batemore the three plastic folders. She looked down at the creased paper and the faded writing which was old-fashioned French, crossed and re-crossed. Without comment she laid the pages in her lap and looked at him.

'Your families,' Keith said, 'have been closely connected by business interests and by occasional marriages for centuries. Between them they own many properties in the Médoc and the Dordogne, including one of the major châteaux. So it's not altogether surprising that when I went on a buying trip through the area I made two separate purchases, each of which was of interest to one or the other of you.

'In the summer of last year, Lady Batemore, you visited your family château to find that your son, Brian, had invited his friends, the Duguidsons, who are remote cousins of yours –'

'Very remote.'

142

'– very remote cousins, to stay there. You terminated that visit and then learned that the young woman, while looking through the family papers in the hope of furthering her studies, had removed a document, that letter which I've just returned to you. Her action drew your attention to the fact that a handsome profit was awaiting you if you could bring two items together.

'The letter was gone, and if you had ever known of its existence you'd hardly be likely to remember its contents. So how did you learn its message without finding out who owned the gun? Because if you had known where to go you would surely have bought it.

'The answer, of course, is through your son. He's as thick as, well, thieves with his very remote cousins. The girl, Valerie, would certainly have boasted about what she was going to do when she got her hands on the money from Chondo's miquelet, but she'd have been a fool to mention Monsieur Detournville's name. Am I right?'

Lady Batemore smiled faintly but made no comment.

'I am, then,' Keith said. 'And you were waiting for him to recover the letter for you. You might have had a long wait, because it seems likely that he had decided to obtain the gun and the letter for himself. Valerie tells me that Brian feels a certain lack of pocket-money. Your interest was purely financial. I don't suppose you're short of this world's goods, but your outgoings must be enormous and we can all use a few extra thousands when they drop into our laps.'

143

Lady Batemore was about to speak but her husband put his hand on her arm. 'Just listen,' he said, 'for the moment.'

'Thank you,' Keith said. 'And then I came barging into this delicately balanced game. I bought Chondo's gun. You told me later that you had no difficulty having my movements traced. So my purchase of Chondo's gun only came to your attention because you were following up the news of my other purchase. These.' Keith leaned forward and lifted the lid of the wooden case. Two saw-handled pistols lay in their fitted places, rusted but deadlier-looking even than Chondo's gun. The case had been superbly fitted and contained, each in its appointed place, a bullet-mould, sprue cutter, patch cutter, nipple-key, loading rods and all the small tools which might be needed to keep the pistols in tune for their deadly trade.

Molly found her voice. 'I don't know what you're talking about,' she said plaintively. 'What did those pistols have to do with Chondo?'

'Damn-all,' Keith said. 'Chondo's miquelet was already in France and half-forgotten before these pistols were made. And yet you probably know more than you think you do. What do you remember about the Rath family scandal?'

Molly's eyes widened. She could not have been married to Keith for six years without learning a great deal about gun history and even coming to share at least some of his enthusiasm. 'One of the last duels in Scotland,' she recited dutifully, 'was fought in eighteen twenty-six. It was hushed up at the time, but it was written up later in several

144

books.' Molly paused. 'Didn't Lord Rath go on to become prime minister?' she asked hesitantly. ' "The evil genius of British politics"?'

'The last one did,' Keith said. 'Go on.'

'All right. He wasn't Lord Rath at the time, he was something else. The elder brother was Lord Rath. The father, who must have ordered the pistols, had popped off a year or two before. Can I call them Big Brother and Little Brother, just to keep them straight?'

'Please do.'

'Well, it was Little Brother who went on to be prime minister. Anyway, there was a party at some castle, I forget which. Some of the men went to play cards, including Little Brother who couldn't really have been old enough for that sort of company. Another man, a distant relative of the Raths from an impoverished branch of the family, accused Little Brother of cheating. Tempers flared, as one of your books puts it. Little Brother was too young to defend his honour so Big Brother, who was notoriously hot-tempered, called the other man out. I forget the other man's name but it began with a C, so I'll call him Cousin.

'They met at dawn, two days later, and Cousin shot Big Brother dead. According to the stories, Cousin climbed straight back into the coach, drove to the coast and took ship to France. But, Keith, are these the Rath pistols?' Molly asked.

'They should be,' Keith said. 'The Rath coat of arms is engraved on the scutcheons.'

'Why would they be walled up in a coach in a barn, then?'

'That's just what I began to wonder as soon as I realized that they were exciting Sir Henry's interest. The whole thing smells like a fix. Cousin ends up in one of the family's French properties. He gets an allowance from Little Brother, who's just copped the title and the family fortune. And, just in case Little Brother decides to do some more elimination of inconvenient relatives, he walls up the coach and the pistols where they'll be safe until he or his successors retrieve them.'

'This is the merest speculation,' Sir Henry said. 'But do continue if it amuses you.'

'It is, it does and I shall,' Keith said.

'But, Keith, could a duel really be rigged?' Molly demanded.

'If the seconds were in it together. Little Brother acted as Big Brother's second. I think it's time we took a look at the evidence. In France I only had time to loosen the pistols – they were rusted to the lining of the case – and to give them a gentle oiling. I was more concerned about having them travel safely than about anything else. I thought that if they'd been sitting around harmlessly for more than a hundred and fifty years they'd do for a little longer. But now I think we'd better have a care.'

Keith took up one pistol, pointing it carefully at the ceiling. 'Beautifully balanced,' he said. With a loading-rod he compared the internal length of the bore with the length from muzzle to nipple. 'Empty, presumably fired,' he said. He did the same with the other pistol. 'Interesting! This one's still loaded.'

Sir Henry looked at him with the eyes of a dead fish. 'I fail to see why you should find that in the least interesting,' he said. 'Even if, which is far from certain, those pistols were last used in a duel – any duel – it would hardly be surprising if the first shot proved lethal and the second pistol were never fired. And another thing. In order to replace skill with chance, it was not unknown for a coin to be tossed in order to decide which participant would fire first.' Sir Henry managed to sound bored. Keith, a practised haggler, could recognize boredom faked to conceal rapt interest.

'Then I'll move on,' Keith said, 'and we'll see whether we find anything more gripping. The hammer's down but there's a cap on the nipple. This is where we find out whether my oil did any good.' Still keeping the muzzle carefully high, Keith put pressure on the hammer. It resisted and then came slowly. He pulled the trigger forward, to ensure that the mechanism was engaged. Then, with a small tool from the case, he detached the percussion cap from the nipple. 'Safe now,' he said.

Molly picked up the cap. 'This cap's been fired,' she said. 'Why didn't the pistol go off? Do you think Little Brother bunged up the vent in the nipple?'

'Let's think about it,' Keith said. He took a nipple-key and a pricker out of the pistol case and started probing with the pricker. 'On the one hand, plugging up the vent might not be certain. And on the other he'd be at risk if Big Brother wanted to see the vent pricked for himself. If he put a spent cap on the nipple, that could also be spotted. The nipple does seem to be bunged up, but you'd expect that after a century and a half in the damp. Well, if it breaks it breaks.'

He fitted the key on to the nipple and applied pressure. The threads resisted, squeaked plaintively and then turned. He took the nipple right out and turned the pistol over. When he probed with the pricker a trickle of powder ran out through the enlarged hole, first grey and then yellow.

'There you are,' Keith said. 'The little beggar loaded his brother's pistol with sand instead of gunpowder. Using a flask with an integral measure, who'd notice?' The case held a single small, copper flask. Keith inverted it over the blotter and pressed the lever of the Sykes Patent Action. A trickle of dark powder spilled on to the white paper. 'Gunpowder,' Keith said. 'He must have palmed a second flask.'

Molly gave an involuntary shiver. 'God save us from relatives,' she said. 'Especially those who're waiting for the cash. But didn't the principals have choice of weapons, rather than the seconds? How would Little Brother know who was going to get which pistol?'

Keith scratched the back of his neck, leaving a dark smear of mixed gun oil and powder smoke. 'Good point,' he said. 'Let's think about it. If Cousin was in the plot he could know which pistol to take – if there's any way to tell them apart. But all the accounts have it that, as things worked out, Cousin was the challenger. Big Brother would have had the choice of weapons. Why would he choose one rather than the other, unless he thought that his baby brother was helping him to steal an advan-

148

tage? . . . Molly, help me look for some visible difference. A bit of engraving, an extra line on the chequering, something like that. Something you can see from the butt end.'

Molly did not even bother to look. 'I already know,' she said.

'You do?'

'I noticed something in France. I took a good look at the engraving, wondering whether it was good enough to photograph for your book. It isn't, by the way. Each of the hammers has a tiny shield engraved on the back of the spur, with a diagonal line across. The lines go different ways.'

Keith looked closely. 'By God, you're right! So the maker identified each pistol, for somebody who knew where to look. Now, why would he do that?' The turnscrews in the pistol case were too short. Keith probed each barrel delicately with his letter-opener. 'I thought so,' he said. 'I bloody well thought so. I've seen a pair like this before. One pistol's smoothbore, the one that's still loaded. The one that was fired has fine rifling almost to the muzzle. It'd throw much straighter. This other one, the smoothbore. . . .' Keith wrapped a strip of paper around the end of a loading-rod until it was a tight fit in the muzzle of that pistol. He drew a bead on the door-handle. 'It's been bored to shoot off to the right,' he said. 'So there you have it. One rigged to miss, the other one bored true and half-rifled.'

Molly looked doubtful. 'If you were having a pistol made,' she said, 'which somebody else might be going to shoot at you, wouldn't you fix it

149

to shoot to his left rather than to his right, your left, where your heart is?'

'I doubt it. When somebody shoots in haste, which he'd be tempted to do in a duel, he's more likely to snatch the trigger and pull right. You wouldn't want the two factors cancelling each other out.'

Sir Henry had been listening with an air of amused indulgence, but now he spoke. 'It may be against my interests to say this,' he said, 'but you've got so far that a little further will hardly matter. Your heart isn't on the left. It's in the centre. You feel it beating on the left because that's where the big arteries are.'

'You see, Clever-clogs?' Keith said.

'Well,' Molly said defiantly, 'if I've understood you properly, Big Brother picked the wrong pistol. Why would he do that?'

Keith frowned. 'You don't go in for easy questions, do you? I can't know everything. I only thought to get this far because the accounts say that there were rumours of a scandal at the time, and then when I bought the pistols everybody seemed to be dashing around like chickens with a fox in the pen; but this is the first chance I've had to study them properly. Let's assume that Little Brother swapped the hammers over. Now, the rigging of the pistols must have been done by the original maker – which might explain why they were ordered from Ross instead of from one of the usual makers of duellers like James Innes or John Thomson. He wouldn't have put the identifying mark on the hammers if there was also a visible

150

identifying mark on the pistols. But a mark would be needed, to ensure that each hammer went back on the proper pistol. Which leads me to think. . . .' With great care and the application of a little force, Keith removed the retaining screw from one of the hammers and, levering gently, removed the hammer from its spindle. 'There we are. The same mark on the lock-plate, hidden by the hammer.' He looked closely. 'And, by God, they've been swapped over. The hammer with the bar sinister belongs on the pistol with the rifling. How appropriate!'

'There's a lovely family for you!' Molly said indignantly. 'Let's see if I've got this straight. Daddy orders a pair of pistols, one of them accurate and one made to miss. His eldest son gets into a duel and grabs the pistol he thinks is going to shoot straight. But his baby brother, who got him into the duel in the first place, has swapped the hammers over so that he picks the wrong one, *and* that one's been loaded with sand so that it won't go off at all. Cousin was part of the conspiracy, and he kept the coach and the pistols together because he didn't trust Little Brother. And,' Molly said, 'I don't blame him. What a family! I can only thank the Lord there are no Raths left in politics.'

There was a brief silence tainted with embarrassment. Keith opened his mouth but again Sir Henry spoke first. He still sounded amused. 'I hate to disillusion you,' he said, 'but Lord Rath – the one to whom you refer as Little Brother – was my great-great-grandfather. He renounced that title in order to stay in the Commons.' Sir Henry turned his attention to Keith. 'Now that you've plumbed this

151

ancient mystery, at least to your own satisfaction, perhaps we could come back to the present?'

Keith wasted a few seconds staring into space while part of his mind returned from history. 'Let's do that,' he said, 'but we'll do it by stages. I spent yesterday afternoon in Register House, filling in the gaps in what I already knew. It seems that Big Brother died unmarried and presumably childless. Little Brother went on to become your great-great-grandfather, Sir Henry. And there was a third and even younger brother who ultimately grew up and became the great-great-*great*-grand-father of the Duguidsons.'

Sir Henry sighed and pretended to hide a yawn. 'I fail to see the relevance,' he said.

'I don't think that you do,' Keith said. 'I intend to pursue it anyway. Somebody tried to kill me and I want to explore the reasoning behind that act. The price I put on these pistols may well be affected.

'Your very remote cousin Valerie Duguidson reads a great deal of relevance into those facts. There seems to have been a family legend that Big Brother had been murdered by Little Brother – a legend which we can now confirm. Little Brother got the family fortune, title and estates. But the law doesn't allow anybody to profit from a crime, and especially not to inherit from somebody they murdered. The inheritance should have passed to the youngest son and have come down to her brother. In her view there has been a hundred and fifty years of injustice which the courts could still put right.'

'She'd be on a loser,' Sir Henry said.

'I told her so, though she seemed unconvinced. I talked to my own solicitor last night. He spoke for about half an hour, mostly in Latin, but if I understood him rightly, the guts of it, in layman's language, is that Little Brother would have been vulnerable, because if the story had come out during his lifetime and if he'd been convicted of murder – which itself is far from certain, because he didn't fire the shot – then the family fortune might have passed to the third brother. But once Little Brother's innocent son had inherited, the inheritance was good.'

Sir Henry studied his fingernails. 'As a statement of the law,' he said, 'that hardly starts to begin to commence. . . . But, in essence, it is correct. In addition there is another factor . . . not exactly a secret although we prefer not to remind people, or each other. My late father was cast in a very different mould from his great-grandfather, the Lord Rath whom you've spent the past hour reviling but who did at least have a very strong capacity for nurturing his own fortune. My father was a gambler. Horses, casinos, the stock exchange, each of them relieved him of what most men would count a fortune. When my turn came to inherit, I found that my inheritance comprised some sadly reduced estates, no money and an encumbrance of debts which equalled or exceeded the value of the land. The money which those young people covet was gone.'

'Ah,' said Keith. Much was explained. He had already noticed that the guns at Wallengreen Castle seemed to have been bought by the yard. This had led him to observe that, while the castle was furnished in period, the pieces were not always a match, which suggested that the castle had been emptied and refurnished.

Sir Henry was frowning, irritated at having had to bare a family wound, but Lady Batemore smiled. 'You are thinking,' she said in her accented and incongruously seductive voice, 'that my husband seems wealthier than would be expected of an out-of-office politician. The answer is simple. I was never a beauty, but I had my attractions. When my husband found his position difficult, he did what members of both families have done when embarrassed. He married a wealthy cousin. My father had been more prudent than Sir Henry's, and my first husband was a member of a great banking family.'

'The salient facts,' Sir Henry said, 'are that, even if such a suit succeeded, the remainder of the Rath fortune is negligible. In any case, as we said, it would not succeed. I explained to my family only last week that the claim is not good in law. I was a barrister before I entered politics,' he added.

Keith thought furiously for a few seconds before he spoke again. Sir Henry, unwittingly, had just added a new dimension to the puzzle. 'Let me think aloud,' Keith said at last. 'We have several groups or individuals with differing reasons for wanting different guns.

'I accept that you, Sir Henry, were only interested in the pistols. You first approached me with an offer for your choice of any two guns. I infer that nobody had told you about Chondo's gun?'

154

'That's so,' Sir Henry confirmed. 'And if anybody had mentioned the matter I should have been uninterested. I never speculate in commodities about which I know nothing. My sole concern was that I would prefer the full depths of my great-great-grandfather's depravity not to be revealed – at least during my lifetime.'

'Thank you,' Keith said. 'Lady Batemore, on the other hand, was prepared to buy three guns, was almost as anxious to buy a single one but was not interested in two. Well, French attitudes tend to set a higher value on money than on scandal. When she learned, through her son, the significance of the letter stolen from her, she realized that there was potential for a substantial profit. The pistols, with their story, would also be valuable, but they could not be resold.

'Then we have the Duguidsons, brother and sister – although I think we need only consider the sister, Valerie. During the summer of last year she abstracted –'

'Stole!' said Lady Batemore.

'– the letter. The Duguidsons are not well heeled. She was trying to raise the wind to buy Chondo's gun when the news broke about the pistols being found in the barn. Well, the rumours that the duel had been rigged have been recorded often enough; as a member of the family she'd certainly know of them. She consulted Mr Threadgold, her neighbour who is also a solicitor. His advice was that she wouldn't stand an earthly chance in court. But she's not a girl to give up easily. She wanted to *know*. It may have been in her mind that, if she could prove

155

the old story, the Batemore family might make a settlement for the sake of her silence.

'At about the same time she heard that her other big chance of money, Chondo's gun, had also fallen into my hands.

'They left for France immediately with a friend, and they made a clever attempt to rob our car of both guns. They failed. So they tried to set me up for blackmail. No attempt on my life was intended – their reactions at the time were enough to tell me that.

'Next into the picture comes another man. I don't know his real name, but he's known, very descriptively, as Creepy Jesus. He's one of the weirdoes who've been infesting the Duguidson house. I know that he was the purchaser of the crossbow. Later, he burgled my house and I caught him. He first denied and then, under some pressure, admitted shooting me. So, who was he working for and what was he after?'

'He could have been working on his own account,' Sir Henry said uninterestedly.

'He could have burgled my house on his own account, but he had no motive for trying to kill me. He claimed that he was after the pistols – which would suggest you as his employer, Sir Henry, if I believed him.'

'But you don't, of course.'

'As it happens, I don't. He tried to lie about everything else, so why should he tell the truth about that? More to the point, I have several pairs of duelling pistols and the best pair hangs in a glass case in my hall – you probably noticed them on your way in. Just before I . . . captured him, he walked past them with only a passing flick of his torch. If he'd been after the Rath pistols he'd surely have stopped and looked.

'His motives were mercenary, pure and simple.

'The Duguidsons don't have any money, except in negligible amounts. They might have offered him a share of what they could get for Chondo's miquelet, but without trade connections it would take them a hell of a time to market a stolen but historic gun. You, on the other hand, have money, but your interest in the pistols is not so great as to induce a rush of spending in one whose reputed vices do not include extravagance.'

Sir Henry nodded slowly. It was almost a bow. His eyes were wary. 'You seem to be eliminating all your runners,' he suggested.

'Not quite. There remain Lady Batemore and her son.'

The temperature, never more than luke-warm, plummeted. Sir Henry paused in the act of lighting a cigar with Keith's table-lighter and rode over his wife's gentler protest. 'If that's an allegation you'd better have something to back it up, or I'll make you sorry.'

'The allegations are still to come,' Keith said. He paused. 'It's funny how errors get perpetuated,' he said at last. 'I do a lot of reading of history, my own specialized area of it. The same tales come up again and again. And when a mistake creeps in, be it a spelling error, a technicality, a date or whatever, it can recur. You can tell who got his facts from whoever else's book. I'm told that it's the same with early copies of the Bible. Now, when Lady Batemore came to my shop she referred to the pistols by C. J. Ross. And that was wrong. The *Scotsman* article only refers to *Ross of Edinburgh*, which agrees with the name on the pistols. There was a C. J. Ross, but he was dead before the pistols were made . . . by his son, Robert Oliver. Nobody else has made that mistake, except Creepy Jesus. Also, you had seen a copy of that article.'

'I have never met the man you refer to by that blasphemous name,' Lady Batemore said. She could have been spitting icicles.

'I never said that you'd met him. I never even thought it. Yet there's a link. Your son Brian mingles freely with the household of his very remote cousins the Duguidsons. He passed on to you all that they thought or did, with only occasional reservations. His Morgan was damaged, so he left it at Bonnyrigg and borrowed one of the family cars for his trip to France. Your car followed ours on to the ferry at Dieppe and an attempt was made to rob our car on the way over. I don't know whether either of you knew what he was up to, and, frankly, I'm not particularly interested. I'll only comment that he must have spun a good yarn before you lent him a valuable car and gave him the money for the trip.'

'He attended to several matters of business for me,' Lady Batemore said.

'I see. A similar car was parked, or rather hidden, near the old quarry just before I was shot at Foleyhill.'

'Are you accusing my son of something?' Lady Batemore demanded. The chill in her beautiful voice was even more bitter. 'If so, what and why?'

158

'Your son,' Keith said, 'has the reputation of being a wild and arrogant young man, but he never lays his own neck on the block. He's a hunt saboteur, but I've never heard of him getting into punch-ups with the hunt followers. He's anti-nuclear, but it's his cousin and not himself that gets had up for bopping a policeman with a placard. He never has tuppence in his pocket, but he charges everything to his stepfather. The picture that came over to me is of a credulous young man, not one of the world's strivers but one who waits for every-thing to fall into his lap and who prefers to avoid taking direct action but to persuade others to act for him.'

'An unkind description, questionable as to fact and to relevance,' Sir Henry said.

'It's relevant background, because it's the picture of a lad who might very well be so concerned about money that he might offer Creepy Jesus a share of the profit if he could help him get his hands on the letter and on Chondo's gun.'

'He'd have the same difficulty,' Sir Henry sugges-ted, 'in selling a stolen antique complete with its provenance.'

His lady rounded on him angrily. 'Henry,' she said, 'you seem to be endorsing this . . . this farrago of nonsense, by taking it seriously!'

'Seriously enough to point out objections as they occur to me. My dear, please believe that this is best left to me.'

'The answer,' Keith said, 'may be that he thought that a private sale to an American collector wouldn't come to my ears. He'd probably have been wrong, if he thought so. On the other hand, I'm very much afraid that my wife may have had the right idea from the start.'

'Me?' Molly said. She was not usually given credit for original thinking.

'Molly suggested that somebody tried to kill me with the crossbow because, if one of the guns we'd bought had been stolen or faked, I'd be the person most likely to spot it. Similarly, with me out of the way Molly wouldn't have known the special significance of any of the guns. And I should point out that, when Creepy Jesus visited us the other night, he was carrying a sawn-off shotgun.'

There was a moment of choking silence. Then Lady Batemore started to protest, but her husband touched her arm and shook his head at her. 'This man Creepy Jesus,' Sir Henry said, 'seems sufficiently endowed with original sin to have acted on his own initiative. If my stepson was in pursuit of one or more guns for financial reasons – which I do not for a moment accept – you have still shown inadequate motive for him to go as far as incitement to murder.'

'Perhaps not,' Keith said. 'You must realize that I'm still thinking aloud. And you only gave me the finishing touch just now when you said that you had explained to your family that, as far as the pistols were concerned, you were bomb-proof, *only last week*. This is how I see it. It was only during my visit to Register House that I realized that Lady Batemore must have been widowed and have remarried while her son was still an infant. He wouldn't have known that the Batemore fortune was exhausted and that the coffers had only been replenished from his mother's and his real father's families. He speaks of you as his father and no doubt thinks of you that way. Male pride being what it is, I doubt if you've ever gone out of your way to enlighten him. He had been living in the pockets of the Duguidsons while Valerie was plotting the overthrow of the house of Batemore, formerly Rath. Valerie would hardly have told him about it, but Creepy Jesus would. And your credulous stepson would have seen the family fortune going up the spout.

'His try at getting the pistols out of my car failed. Hugh Duguidson was in my shop while I was telling my partner that the guns were coming by water. The Duguidsons decided to get me into a compromising situation and to blackmail me. Hugh Duguidson took Creepy Jesus up to Foleyhill to kill the deer, and, I suppose, took him home again. Brian brought Creepy back to Foleyhill in your Jag., and waited round the back of the quarry while Creepy went up and hid until I arrived and he could nail me, leaving the Duguidsons stuck with the problem. The Duguidsons weren't quite so ruthless. They tied up my wound and phoned for an ambulance or I wouldn't be here now.

'By the time the guns landed in this country, you'd pointed out that Valerie was living in a fantasy world and that the pistols wouldn't mean a damn thing in court. Maybe that was a relief to him. But he'd had a taste of violence and of the prospect of money. He was getting up a head of steam. Anything went, as long as there was no apparent risk to himself. This was his chance to get off the short financial rein. If he could bring together Chondo's gun, the letter and if possible a corroboration from Monsieur Detournville, he could be independent. With the help of Creepy Jesus, of course.'

Lady Batemore was struggling to get out of her chair, despite Sir Henry's grip on her arm. Her voice was no longer seductive, but high and venomous. 'Can you prove any of this?' she demanded. 'If you can't, and if you repeat a word of it outside this room, you can expect an action for slander.'

'I'm not trying to prove anything at this stage,' Keith said, 'and I don't have to. The police have the facilities, and its their job to protect me. If this is an unsolved mystery and there seems to be any likelihood of my still being in danger, then the sensible thing for me to do is to take what I now know and suspect to the police. You know young Brian's character and his movements better than I do. Judge for yourselves. If I start the police on a further investigation, what do you think they'll find out?'

'That's what you get, Adèle, for not taking my advice,' Sir Henry said coldly. 'I suggest that you go and wait in our very comfortable car while I finish my discussion with Mr Calder in private. Leave the letter with me.'

Lady Batemore got up and stumped out of the room.

'I think I hear Deborah crying,' Molly said quickly. She hurried into the calm security of her kitchen.

162

By the time Keith had, at long last, seen Sir Henry to his car and waved the Batemores on their way, he was ravenous. Molly had laid the table in the kitchen. She put down a late and hasty lunch in front of him and sat down opposite with her own. 'How did you make out with Sir Henry?' she asked.

'Not too bad,' Keith said with his mouth full. 'God, I'm hoarse. I haven't spoken so much since we got married.'

'Don't be sarcastic. Just tell me all about it.'

Keith decided that he would not want Molly to burst with curiosity, not in the newly-decorated kitchen. He took pity. 'Sir Henry was after the pistols. Although the Rath story is well enough known, he didn't want the full and dirty details coming to light with an election not too far off. He also wasn't averse to capitalizing on the value of the Louisiana letter. I told him that no way was he getting the pistols at his sort of price, but that, with my part of the whole package, I'd throw in an undertaking to hold on to them and not publish anything while he's still active in politics. By which time, with the whole story told, they should be worth a mint.'

'That could be years,' Molly said. 'Wallace won't be pleased. You're just adding those pistols to your private collection.'

'I don't have a private collection. And politicians' careers don't last forever. He'll be out on his ear soon enough. Anyway, we struck a deal in the end. He gives me his two guns and the letter and I keep the pistols a secret and cut him in for a share of the net profit on Chondo's gun – *after* a deduction for

163

part of all our travelling expenses and so on. And he'd better not hold his breath waiting for his share, because I mean to jack up its value by writing articles about it over the next year or two.' Keith smiled to himself. He was secretly amused at the thought that Sir Henry's share would be diminished by a proportion of the value of the drink which he had brought back from France.

'You're a swick,' Molly said, without even divining Keith's secret thought. 'So now we know the whole story?'

'Do we hell! We have a tacit agreement not to probe any further.'

They cleared their plates in silence. Molly passed the bowl of fruit. 'But it can't all be over,' she said suddenly. 'Not just like that. I mean, people have conspired to try to rob and blackmail. And if it was Creepy Jesus who tried to kill you, somebody else put him up to it.'

'What really bugs me,' Keith said, 'is that I handled Creepy Jesus all wrong. I'd have got much more out of him if I'd realized that he was actually *enjoying* being roughed up in the presence of a moderately attractive old lady in her flannel nightie.'

Molly ignored the insults. 'What you've really been saying is that, while Sir Henry thought he was driving a hard bargain and you knew that you were robbing him blind, you were both happy enough that the police don't know anything and there's no legal proof of any of it and you don't want the boat rocked.'

Keith wished that Molly would develop enough

164

savoir faire to avoid saying uncomfortable truths out aloud. 'Yes,' he said.

'Well, what about Lady Batemore's son? He seems to have been the evil genius, the behind-the-scenes baddie.'

'The rat in the arras,' Keith agreed. 'Sir Henry promised me that the lad wouldn't come back to Britain, and I said that if I ever got wind of young Batemore being in this country, under that or any other name, I'd produce a witness who'd seen him going up Foleyhill with a crossbow.'

'Keith, you didn't!' Molly did not sound displeased. 'What was Sir Henry's reaction to that?'

'He seemed to think it perfectly reasonable. Which, from his point of view, it probably was. You've got to remember that, with an election to come at any time, a murderous great-great-grandfather might be mildly embarrassing but a stepson on a serious charge would be a disaster. And there's another side to it. I gathered that he rather expected her ladyship to decide that, if her baby boy was to be exiled, it was her duty to join him. Which seems tough on young Batemore for all his misdeeds, but Sir Henry seemed to think of it as a good idea. I think he sees himself taking up residence in a Westminster flat, pending Number Ten falling vacant, and being kept warm by a dolly-bird secretary or a Turkish wrestler, whichever happens to turn him on. I wouldn't know anything about that.'

Molly was not interested in Sir Henry's preferences. 'Whatever anybody else thinks, Sir Henry was ready enough to believe that his stepson was behind you getting shot,' she said. Then another thought hit her. She tried not to let her excitement show. 'You think he'll be giving up Wallengreen Castle?'

'Probably,' Keith said. 'But if you're beginning to imagine us taking it over, put the idea out of your tiny mind. Good God, I've not finished paying for this place yet.'

'Of course.' Molly filed the subject away for future reference. She had absolute faith in Keith's ability to achieve any goal which she could motivate him to set for himself. 'What about Creepy Jesus?' she asked.

'Abroad, by now, and out of reach. I'm sure of it. If the police had got him, we'd have heard.'

'Everybody happy,' Molly said, 'except the Duguidsons. Do they get anything out of it?'

'They get rid of Creepy Jesus, who can't have been much fun to have around. I can't think of anything else. Except that I think we might do them a favour.'

'Favour?' Molly tried not to sound suspicious.

'If your brother and I went up to Foleyhill for a couple of days and nights, with sleeping bags, a pair of silenced two-twos, infra-red lamps and some Fenn traps, we could transform that place. These idealists mean well, but they've been brain-washed by Walt Disney. They think that you've only got to give the cuddly bunnies somewhere safe where nasty people can't get at them and they'll live happily ever after. What usually happens, just as it has at Foleyhill, is that the place gets taken over by vermin, especially by those that prey on other creatures' eggs or young. When they've cleaned out their own patch they go raiding over the boundary. We could improve the place out of recognition and they'd never know they'd been visited.'

Molly smiled sweetly. 'Get down off your soapbox,' she said. 'What's in it for you?'

'Just a public-spirited concern for the wildlife of the district, and a selfless desire to help the Duguidsons and make life sweeter for the farmers and shoot-owners round about.'

'All right,' Molly said, sighing. 'So when do I expect you to disappear, leaving me to placate Wallace, help out in the shop and be ready with an alibi?'

'Oh, not for ages. I'll want to take expert advice before I rock the ecological boat. We'd be safer from interruption when the December exams are on. And,' Keith added, 'by then the foxes should have their winter pelts.'

'Ha!' Molly pointed her finger into his face. 'You old bastard! It's just that you miss the old poaching days. Admit it!'

Keith bit the tip of her finger, gently, and left the room without replying.

He was back in five minutes. 'Talking of poaching, have you seen my desk-lighter?'

'The one you made out of the powder-testing flintlock thing?'

'The éprouvette. Yes. It's vanished.'

'Oh, Keith. Don't say that the Duguidsons have pinched it!'

'That was my first thought,' Keith said. 'But,

after they'd been and gone, don't I remember Sir Henry using it?'

Molly was horrified. 'He just wouldn't do a thing like that,' she declared. 'He's a *politician*.'

'I know you believe in Santa Claus,' Keith said. 'But is there no end to your simple faith? An honest man's chance of getting elected to Parliament is about the same as of winning the pools. This is his way of getting back at me. I made out that there was another way I could authenticate Chondo's gun. He knew I was bluffing, but he couldn't call it. Then, when I promised that I'd hang on to the pistols during his political career, I added something about not doing anything to shorten that career. He smiled at that, and I thought it was because there wouldn't have been anything I could do to shorten it anyway. But now I think that he was smiling because he knew that, after saying what I'd just said, I couldn't run straight to the police and accuse him of theft.'

'Well, I think that's awful,' Molly said. 'That thing's a valuable antique.'

'In point of fact, it isn't. It's something I made during my apprenticeship, out of odds and ends.'

'Oh. So what are you going to do?'

'For the moment, just what he knew I'd do. Nowt.'

Wallace, when Keith saw him that evening, seemed uncharacteristically uninterested in the details of Keith's deal with Sir Henry. Other things were pressing on his mind.

'That goddam bloody awful McSwale & Angus gun,' he said. 'It's been a lesson to me. Never, ever again will I try and do your job for you.'

'It wasn't all that bad,' Keith said, trying to keep his voice steady. 'You described it as knicker-pink, or some such words. But I saw what was left of it when the cop picked it up off the floor and it was a much nicer pink. About the colour of an angel's tit.' He spluttered with laughter.

Wallace ground his teeth and made faces. 'You think it's bloody funny? Well, laugh this off. The finish was much admired at Lord Whatsit's shoot. A retired admiral who was there has brought in a McSwale & Angus of his own. He wants it refinished in the authentic Jock McSwale colour.'

Keith stopped laughing. 'You didn't really use that story, did you? You'll get the firm a bad name if you take my little jokes seriously.'

'I didn't take it seriously. I just couldn't think of another excuse. And Mr Threadgold's been on the phone. When he gets his gun back he wants it re-barreled and finished in the same colour.'

'Well, you did it once and you can do it again.'

'The trouble is that I can't. I've been trying it out on bits of off-cut, and I c-come up with a different bloody colour every time.'

'Then you'll just have to tell them that our expert, the only man who knew how to do it, just died, and the secret with him.'

'Ain't it the truth?' Wallace said unhappily.

CHAPTER ELEVEN

Time, in its usual way, rolled past almost un-heeded.

Keith forgot the Duguidsons and the Batemores except when isolated incidents reminded him.

The first of his articles about Chondo and the miquelet brought in several substantial offers for the gun. With Wallace's reluctant agreement, Keith refused them all. There was a lot more mileage to be gained.

Creepy Jesus seemed to have dropped off the face of the earth, regretted by none.

Keith was making a study of percussion guns prior to the invention of the centre-fire cartridge. He repaired and cleaned up Sir Henry's Maynard tape-primer gun, and added it to his catalogue at a price at least double what he expected any collector to pay, thus demarking it as part of the personal collection which he always denied having. A sudden fluctuation in rates of exchange caught him out. A Belgian millionaire collector bought it at the catalogue figure. Keith was furious. Wallace did a little dance down the middle of the shop, accompanying himself with a creditable imitation of

Woody Woodpecker, to the great alarm of an old lady who was buying waders for her grandson at the time.

Keith was restored to general health at a speed which confounded the doctors. The tenderness of his shoulder was another matter. By December it was abating and he managed his excursion to Foley-hill with his brother-in-law. The recoil of anything heavier than a small-bore rifle bothered him for several more months. He contented himself with some outings to decoy pigeon within the range of a four-ten shotgun, and then graduated to rabbiting with his heavy magnum twelve-bore allied with lightly-loaded Impax cartridges – an unhandy combination but comfortably devoid of kick.

By the return of the shooting season, however, he was back on form, all disability forgotten.

And then, rather more than a year after the visits of the Duguidsons and the Batemores to Briesland House, a General Election was called. Government changed hands.

'Look at this, will you?' Keith asked. He and Wallace were relaxing in the study at Briesland House over a large dram apiece, following a protracted business discussion which had ranged also over women, football and, of course, shooting.

Wallace accepted the magazine and followed Keith's finger. The glossy photograph showed Home Secretary Sir Henry Batemore, aglow with fresh pride, seated in his new office. A few personal effects, carefully chosen and artfully arranged, decorated the desk before him. Prominent among these was Keith's éprouvette. It had the appearance of a truncated flintlock pocket pistol, the barrel being replaced by a powder container, spring and small quadrant.

'He's got a b-bloody nerve,' Wallace said.

'He has. And it raises some interesting implications. I told you that I promised I wouldn't do anything to shorten his political career?'

'Several times, in t-tones ranging from fury to disgust.'

'When I made that gadget, I had a hell of a job hiding the gas container where it wouldn't show. But it's a good, big container and won't need filling very often, so it didn't seem to matter that it was held by lots of tiny grub-screws. Well, that old bugger only seems to smoke the occasional cigar, so the gas might have lasted for years. But on his desk in the Home Office it's going to get used. And when the gas runs out he's going to have to take it to somebody, probably a jeweller, to refill it for him.'

'And so?'

'So here's where it gets interesting. Whoever takes it apart is going to find something like this.' Keith took the ink-wells off his desk-set and handed the base to Wallace. Neatly impressed across the underside were the words *Stolen from Keith Calder*, and the phone number of Briesland House.

'It's my form of therapy,' Keith said. 'Any time I feel nervous or depressed, or when I stop for thought, I look around for something personal which I'm not going to want to sell again, and stamp my identity on it. There's probably some deep,

172

psychological reason which I'd rather not know about.'

'The jeweller will only phone Sir Henry.'

'I'm not so sure. Jewellers and gunsmiths have to keep their noses very clean when it comes to stolen goods. If I found a message like that inside a gun, say, I'd phone the number even if the gun had been brought to me by Her Majesty in person.'

'All right,' Wallace said. 'Suppose the phone rings and a voice asks you whether you've lost a desk-lighter made out of a reproduction éprouvette. What then?'

'If I'm asked,' Keith said slowly, 'I think I'm morally bound to pass it off.'

'And if Molly takes the call.'

'That,' Keith said, 'is the crunch question. She didn't give any promises and I haven't told her not to implicate Sir Henry. I reported the loss to the police at the time, letting them jump to the conclusion that Creepy Jesus had pinched it and that I'd only just discovered the loss. Molly's still furious over it. If she was asked whether Sir Henry was here between Creepy Jesus's visit and our discovery of the theft, she'd swear to it like a shot.'

'You'd be breaking your word if you gave evidence. As if you cared.'

'Molly didn't give her word. And it's her lighter. I made her a present of it, never mind when.'

Wallace thought over this sophistry. 'He'd be forced to resign. They couldn't have the Home Secretary prosecuted for theft. And he couldn't be allowed to shelter behind his status as head of the police.'

'That's right.'

'You've fairly got it in for him.'

'That photograph didn't include my lighter by accident,' Keith said. 'He's taunting me. Besides, I want to get on with publishing my material on the Rath pistols.'

CHAPTER TWELVE

A fortnight or so later, Keith announced that the moon and tides were approaching perfection and that the weather forecast indicated ideal conditions for a morning's recreation – stormy, with a probability of low cloud.

Molly went to look out his wildfowling gear, pausing only to remark that he just had to be out of his mind.

Keith could understand her comment, even if he could not agree with it, as he breakfasted next morning in the very small hours and set off on a long drive to the coast. The car lurched and shuddered in a blustery wind and the wipers had to cope with occasional sleet from clouds that were hiding the hill tops. Keith gripped the wheel and nodded to himself. The geese would not be in a hurry to climb in such weather.

He came at last to a broad estuary which had been one of his hunting grounds for twenty years and turned off on to a farm-track which led him, jolting, to a favourite parking place a hundred yards from the high water mark. An old van already occupied half the space, its bonnet still warm. So there was a chance of company out on the flats.

In the lee of the car, Keith dressed in his warmest clothes and put oilskins on top. He checked his gear carefully and set off. Even Brutus, his labrador, seemed daunted by the weather and stayed close as they slithered their way out over the mud. It was almost pitch dark, the last light of a setting moon coming faintly beneath the scudding clouds. Keith pressed on, guided by the wind behind his shoulder and urged on by the music of geese ahead, a thousand or more by the sound. He angled across to intercept their likeliest line of flight.

A dark shape came out of the darker night, half a tree and a tangle of branches all cast up by the tide. It was not perfect camouflage, but it would do. Keith and Brutus settled into concealment. Keith felt a breathless surge of excitement, a taste of the old magic. Wallace and he shot as often as the business would allow, perhaps oftener. But there was no quarry to match a goose on the foreshore.

Dawn, when it came, arrived without warning. At one moment Keith could only make out the difference between earth and sky, and then, it seemed only seconds later, he could see the gulleys and rivulets in the mud, the scatterings of weed and driftwood and the dark specks of a multitude of geese.

The note of the chorus changed as the birds became restless. The making tide was beginning to disturb them. Keith slipped his safety-catch off and breathed deeply.

176

A trio of mallard, always the first in flight, came over from behind. He was almost caught napping but he snapped off a shot and a duck turned over and dropped. At a nod from Keith, Brutus was away, bolting over the mud with his tail thrashing, to return in a few seconds, filthy but ecstatic.

The shot had disturbed the geese. The chattering changed its tone again and group after group took to the air. Keith felt his usual sense of wonder and frustration as the majority defied his best guess, either by turning more quickly and passing to his right, or by rising for longer in the teeth of the wind and coming over him high out of shot. Then at last one small skein of yelping pinkfeet came straight for him, rising steadily but still in range. At the last moment Keith stood up and took out the leader. The skein broke, swung and re-formed on a new leader. With his other barrel Keith took a second bird. He restrained Brutus. Both his geese were stone dead and there might be more to come.

The sound of a third shot came to him, attenuated by the wind, but not from far away. A third goose fell from the same skein. He could see nobody. The goose hit the ground but it was still struggling. He was on the point of sending Brutus to bring it for the *coup-de-grâce* when a black and white collie erupted from an invisible depression in the mud and raced forward to collect the wounded bird.

A few minutes later it was all over. The sands were bare and the geese had gone to their feeding grounds on the farmland. Keith might have stayed on for the chance of a late teal, but time was precious and Christmas dinner was already in the bag. Also, the tide was making fast. He sent Brutus after his geese and stood up.

Full daylight had arrived, unnoticed.

Away to his left another figure rose out of the mud.

Keith accepted one goose from Brutus and set off. The use of a collie for retrieving caught his curiosity. There are no rules, only tradition and breeding, to determine which dog does which job, and indeed Keith knew of the pair of Victorian gamekeepers who had trained a pig to retrieve. All the same, he fancied a chat about it. There was always more to learn. He angled across to intercept the other fowler.

The sleet, which had let up, was falling again. When their paths met, Keith rolled up his balaclava and the stranger unwound a heavy scarf, each showing his face. The other man was in his early twenties, short but sturdily built, with a round face and freckles which had not shown up in the photographs. Keith recognized him immediately but kept his face blank.

The young man took one look and stopped dead. 'I know you,' he said. 'You're Keith Calder.'

Keith stooped to take his second goose from a panting Brutus while he decided that circumspection would pay no dividends. 'I know you too,' he said.

'You saw me coming down from Foleyhill with the Duguidsons. I've been thinking I owed you an explanation, but I kept putting it off until it seemed o'er late. My name's Carluke, but I'd feel better about it all if you called me Andy.'

They shook hands, exchanging foreshore slime.

'Would you fancy some breakfast?' Andy asked. 'I farm just over the hill there.'

Keith hesitated.

'Bacon, egg, sausages, mushrooms. And I think there's kidneys.'

The kidneys swung it. Keith accepted.

Keith followed the rusty van up a side road and over the brow of a hill chequered with the brown and green of mixed farming. The collie showed signs of territorial defensiveness so he left Brutus in the car.

'Come through into the kitchen,' Andy said. 'Hang your things to dry. If you like to start the fry-up while I do the first chores we'll have time for a crack.'

A start had been made to redecoration, but Keith noticed the signs that comfort and convenience over-rode appearances, which suggested that Andy was a bachelor and living alone.

Twenty minutes later they were digging into the sort of second breakfast which makes up for the rigours of wildfowling.

'I think I feel survival creeping up on me,' Keith said.

'My dad has a bigger place a few miles off,' Andy explained between mouthfuls. 'There's only a hundred acres here. Dad's getting on now. If I make a success of this place on my own, he'll think about retiring and leaving me to carry on. I'm getting wed in the New Year.'

'To Valerie Duguidson?'

'God, no! I'm back to my childhood sweetheart. You guessed that I was overboard for Valerie?'

'I saw you frisking around her, coming down from Foleyhill. I put you down as a casual helper, a hanger-on looking for her favours. Was I wrong?'

Andy sighed and shook his head. 'You weren't wrong.'

'Even so, how could you, a shooting man, join up with a bunch of antis and go in for sabotaging somebody else's shoot? And you from a farming background!' Even to himself, Keith sounded priggish.

'I'm not proud of it,' Andy admitted. 'I was at the Agricultural College, and I was kicked out of my digs. My landlady fancied me, but I couldn't stand the sight of her. I could have fancied her daughter, though. The only place I could find, just at the end of the academic year and the middle of the tourist season, was at the Duguidsons. I could hardly thole some of the weirdies who hung out there, but it was a roof. And Val was something else. Sophisticated. And legs up to here.'

'I've seen them.'

'Aye, so you have. All the way. Then you can guess the effect she'd have on a lad just off the farm. I thought she was the tops. For me, the sun shone out of her fud. Well, you've seen and it doesn't,' he added. 'She was aye sounding off about the wrong that was done her great-great-granddad, or who-ever it was, and how there was an old tale in the family that whoever got the pistols could prove it. So when they wanted an extra driver, I went along. I didn't know they meant to steal the things, but if I had known I don't suppose it'd've made any difference. It was a lark, a crusade, a holiday, and doing something for my bird. She was spitting feathers when she found you didn't have them in the car with you.'

'Birds –' Keith began.

'All right, birds don't spit feathers. But she's more like a cat. Sleek, demanding, determined to get her own way.

'I knew nothing of their plan to fit you up, not at the time. Even in the state I was in, I don't think I'd have stood still for that. You weren't meant to be hurt, you know.'

'So they kept telling me,' Keith said.

'Well, you weren't. I was in the house all that day, doing some reading. I heard that somebody'd had an accident, and they asked Creepy whether he'd been out again. He said that he hadn't, which was a bloody lie, but it didn't seem to be any business of mine so I kept mum. I was going off their ideas by then anyway, so I wanted to stay loose.'

'You didn't seem to have gone off their ideas that day I saw you at Foleyhill,' Keith said.

The boy flushed. 'I still had the hots for Valerie. For a while, what they said about animal rights seemed to make a sort of sense. Then, when I came to think about it, I tried to imagine a world in which animals had rights of the kind they were talking about. It just didn't make any sense at all, and a farmer was the person to see it. I just went along that day to please Valerie, and for the lark, and because they bet me I couldn't work old Tessa from cover.' The collie, recognizing her name, made a push at his leg.

181

'I'd have bet you couldn't get her to retrieve,' Keith said. He thought back. 'If you were in Bonnyrigg all that day when I got shot, you might be able to confirm something for me. The second time that Creepy Jesus went out, was it Brian Batemore who picked him up?'

'No,' Andy said, 'it was not. I was just coming back from taking Tessa a walk and I saw Creepy getting into a blue Jag. Brian's dad was driving. There was nobody else in the car.'

The kitchen was warm with the range burning. Keith had been near to dozing off, but this jerked him awake. 'Sir *Henry* was driving?'

Andy let Keith sit in silence while he turned his ideas over. He could believe in Sir Henry as the mastermind behind any number of evils. But why?

'Sir Henry was after the pistols,' Keith said at last. 'But he already knew that they had no legal importance, not the way Valerie imagined. They show that Sir Henry's ancestor was a bad, bad bugger, a fratricide among other things. But that information would be no more than an embarrassment. I doubt whether any politician, or any other man, would come out well if every one of his nineteenth-century forebears was brought into the light of day. I just can't see him going to such lengths to get his hands on the pistols.'

Andy poured two more mugs of tea that was now almost black and only lukewarm. 'I'll have to get to work soon,' he said. 'Meantime, I don't know the answer. You likely know more about it than I do. But I'll tell you this. Brian and Val and

Hugh and Sir Henry, they're all related, aren't they?'

'Not very closely.'

'That doesn't matter. I've been around the breeding of cattle all my life and I know that what matters is the way the genes come out. The three that I know all think the same way, and from what I hear Sir Henry's no different. Once one of that lot sets their mind to a thing they don't give up and they'll go to any lengths to get what they want. And if they don't get it, they'll take some petty revenge.'

This was so consistent with what Keith already knew that he only nodded.

'Sir Henry, now,' Andy went on. 'From what Brian says, he cares about nothing in the world except his political career and the power and glory that it brings him. If he thinks the way those others do, once he made up his mind to get those things because they just might count against him, he'd soon forget their relative unimportance and go after them hell-bent. Just the same way, from what I read in the papers, as he's got on in politics by going hell-bent after every political objective along the way.'

Keith decided that he very much disliked what he was hearing. 'If he ever makes it to prime minister like his great-great-granddad. . . .'

'He'll be just the same sort of disaster. He'd declare war on China if it'd win him a by-election.' Andy hesitated and scratched his ear. 'Look, I'm going to tell you one more thing. I've been swithering over telling it, and I'm almost feared to say it aloud. And, mind, I'm never going to repeat it to another soul, let alone give it in evidence.

'There was one night, just before I found new digs and moved. I'd been out late at a student party and when I got to my room Creepy came to talk to me. He was a man I'd no use for at all, but for some reason he'd taken to me. He was excited. Something had happened, and I think he'd been drugging. He'd come to say goodbye, and to get my help lugging some of his books and junk out of the house. He said he was in real trouble with the police, but he'd been on the phone to Brian's dad, who was going to get him out of the country. He had friends in a hippy colony in Spain and he was going to go to them until he'd "got it together" again. I helped him to lug his stuff down the road to where he was going to be picked up. As I left, I saw Sir Henry arrive again in the blue Jag.'

'I was always sure it was Sir Henry that got him out of the country,' Keith said.

'And I'm sure you're wrong,' Andy said grimly. 'I don't think Creepy ever left the country. Another lad who'd been with us in Bonnyrigg went out to Spain for a month last summer. He called in here just lately, to bum a bed and a few quid. He said that Creepy never arrived in Spain.'

Keith spent another half hour questioning Andy Carluke, without managing to learn anything more. He gave up and made his farewells.

Andy came with him to the car. 'Any time you're over this way after the geese,' he said, 'drop in for breakfast.'

184

'Don't think that I won't.'

'You heard that Foleyhill won a conservation award?'

Keith laughed wryly. 'I hadn't, but good luck to them anyway.'

'They mean well,' Andy said. 'And they worked at it.'

The road was treacherous and the car, labouring against a wind which was determined to shake it off the road, was skittish, but Keith drove without concentrating. There was too much on his mind.

His previous ideas, he now realized, were no more than theories, confirmed only by the words of those who were best suited to them. Instead of belief, he now had certain knowledge. Sir Henry Batemore, on top of his other sins, had destroyed Creepy Jesus.

Keith wiped mist from the windscreen, adjusted the heater and scowled out at a grey and white world. He decided that nothing on earth would induce him to accuse Sir Henry of conspiracy to murder. There was no physical evidence; the charge would depend on the testimony of Andy Carluke, who had already refused to give it; of the Duguidsons whose interest might well be in silence; and of Creepy Jesus who was no longer in a position to testify to anything except the existence or otherwise of a life after death. The very thought of being the man who had unsuccessfully accused the Home Secretary of murder made Keith's intestines cringe.

He found, to his surprise, that while he was disapproving he was not in the least shocked. He had met with murder before and had nearly been its victim. On one occasion he had had full knowledge of the murder of a blackmailer by a victim who had been manoeuvred into a vulnerable position and then pressured beyond endurance; and Keith had helped to bury for ever the evidence of that deed. He did not hold all human life to be sacred, not even his own; although, if he had had to think about it, he might have perceived sanctity in the lives of Deborah and Molly.

But if Keith could condone murder in the abstract, the circumstances surrounding the death of Creepy Jesus he found unforgivable. It had been mean and unnecessary, a mere precaution against the chance of a loose tongue; and it had been committed, or at the very least ordered, by a man in a position of power, a contender for the highest office in the government and a man, moreover, who had shown almost a genius for predicting the reactions of others. Such a man would, quite literally, get away with murder. And if ever he were esconced in Number Ten. . . .

Snow was lying across the road on the high ground above Newton Lauder, and the tail of the car skidded suddenly. Keith was jerked back from his reverie and wrenched the wheel. The car whipped the other way, and again he caught it. This time he retained control and drove on, more attentively. His heart was thumping.

When he was on clear road again he let his mind drift back on to his previous line of thought. Either the respite or the surge of adrenalin had swirled away the mists, leaving the issues clear. Sir Henry Batemore was not to be trusted with power. He was guilty of a heinous crime, although the chances of his ever being convicted of it were negligible. But for a Home Secretary to stand accused, on incontrovertible evidence, of a petty crime must at the very least damage his chances of higher office. His petty gesture of revenge would be his undoing. He had taunted Keith by placing the éprouvette tablelighter in the forefront of his official photograph, confident that Keith would feel bound by his promise. Keith, having come well out of their business dealings, would have let the matter go . . . but for the killing of Creepy Jesus.

Keith slapped the steering wheel and nearly lost the car again. 'I'll connach the bastard,' he told himself aloud.

CHAPTER THIRTEEN

He was spared any agonizing over breaking his word. He returned to Briesland House, intending to change into clothes suitable for relieving Wallace at the shop. He found Molly, as she would have put it 'up to High Do'.

'There was a man on the phone,' she said breathlessly. 'He was speaking from London, one of those posh shops in Piccadilly. He asked whether you'd lost an ornament.'

Deborah looked up from her picture book. 'Onnalmink,' she confirmed.

'What did you say?' Keith asked.

'I described the éprouvette thing,' Molly said defiantly. 'I said that it had been taken. He said that it had been brought in for attention and what did I want him to do about it? I told him I'd call him back. Keith, what're you going to do?'

'I'm not going to do a damn thing,' Keith said. 'It was your lighter and you're the one who said you'd call back. Do whatever you'd do if it was just up to you.'

'If it was just up to me I'd tell him to take it straight to the police.'

There was a brief silence.

'Well, I've got two geese to bring in from the car,' Keith said. 'And a duck.'

Deborah scrambled to her feet. 'I come fetch'm,' she said. Her parents were beginning to wonder whether she didn't think that she was a labrador.

Keith had expected an infinity of repercussions ranging from police harassment to an action for defamation.

In the event, the matter was handled with such discretion that it was almost an anticlimax. Sir Henry, it seemed, had made himself hated at all levels in the police and also in Downing Street. Chief Inspector Munro, who had learned the facts through some police grapevine, told Keith later that the allegation had found its way rapidly to a very senior police officer who had taken it straight to the office of the Prime Minister.

Sir Henry Batemore was allowed to retire on grounds of ill-health. He took up residence on his wife's estates in France, where he was again much disliked.

Wallengreen Castle was bought by an Italian industrialist.

Creepy Jesus never knew what an upheaval had been precipitated in his memory. He had met an Argentine heiress of great wealth and singular ugliness and the two were living in Casablanca, eternally stoned out of what was left of their minds.

Postscript

Newton Lauder is a fictitious town somewhere between the Pentlands and the Cheviots. Its inhabitants and the other characters in the book are wholly fictitious.

I have tried to be accurate in all factual matters but acknowledge that I have taken mild liberties with history: the antique guns which figure in this story do not exist, but they could have done. I also admit to simplifying the necessary procedures for gaining access to the information stored in the Police National Computer.

G.H.